NINETEEN
LANDINGS

BOOK 2

Q Taylor

NINETEEN LANDINGS
BOOK 2

iUniverse books may be ordered through booksellers or by contacting:

iUniverse
1663 Liberty Drive
Bloomington, IN 47403
www.iuniverse.com
844-349-9409

ISBN: 978-1-6632-1662-5 (sc)
ISBN: 978-1-6632-1663-2 (e)

Library of Congress Control Number: 2021900814

Print information available on the last page.

iUniverse rev. date: 01/13/2021

To Holly
&
John

CONTENTS

THE 8TH LANDING

CHILDREN OF THE LAST

In the aftermath of drastic climate change and global warming, years after the senseless nuclear wars of mankind, there was a global shutdown period in which the dwindling remaining humans named, "The Great Light Age"; when the Suns solar flares reign supreme for years upon the earth. Now, only a small portion of humanity cling to its existence and what remains of this so called life. Scattering across the earth, surviving among the dead and dying, great plains of the world, man fight against its own destruction as the planet continue to grow and thrive in the colliding solar system. The Earth, reclaims itself victorious against the virus that once claimed, infected and reshaped it.

Where a technologically advanced and highly populated country once flourished, a vast cooked and radiated desert of enormous dunes bury the past, along with old states and historical cities. Once more, the planet forces life's hand upon natural selection which always chooses the strongest and most adaptive to survive. Here, in an Oasis of nothingness, the dry sky glimmers without the presence of birds, over land, absence for miles of insect life. Prints of deceased scavengers disappear in the dirt inside the uncovered ruins of a forgotten, lost and abandoned city against the skeletal, rusted, metal frames of once mighty sky scrapers and other large, brick structures that fall to waste among the rubble and sand within the barren landscape of the new wasteland. Looking even closer, an even smaller set of human tracks, fresh, Human and more recent, continue into a small burrow which led to an open window of a collapsed, crumbling building, poking out from a hillside of sand.

Covered in grime and dirt, a pair of dark human hands ravage among the trash and old office furniture of the building; a pair of large eyes peer from the opening of old tattered garments. Raised during the end of the Religion war, a young, dark haired survivor, now scavenger named Destin, desperately searches for food rations and water. "Come on, give me something, give me something!" Under a lighter, the young man pulls back a hood revealing a dirt covered face. Finding nothing edible, he searches through a desk drawer and cabinets toppled over along a wall. "Empty." He moves to what appears to be the main door and enters into a hall of glass dividers which separates the room from other small offices. The sun beam rays of light through small holes in the ceiling and caved in walls which help to guide Destin to a nearby window where he eyes something familiar; two interesting old machines sitting in the shadows against the far wall. "Alright, a liquid in a can machine, and a ration holder!" He mutters to himself. Wiping his mouth anxiously, Destin opens a filthy, forest green duffle bag, pulls out a long iron pipe, and smashes through the windows of two old vending machines. Loading up ancient old sodas and a few bags of snacks that remained into an old leather book bag on his back; a movement of a shadow passing over one of the small openings of light from outside raises alarm. Having not seen another living soul in seasons; Destin quickly scrambles back to the surface to take a closer look.

Bright and dry, the region had begun to embark upon the new coldest season in history as heavy clouds, not yet thick enough to block out the Sun, begin to blow in from the west. Shading his eyes from the brightness of the day, Destin raises his hood and covers his mouth with a sand scarf, protecting him from the chilled, sandy winds. Lowering a pair of sun specs, he scans the area. Seeing no one for miles, Destin glances down at the sight of fresh footprints in the sand. Heart racing in excitement and growing curiosity, he is snatched backwards by the scruff of his neck, and mouth forced open by the barrel of a large gun. Destin's muffled voice is silenced as a large and powerful hand cocks the man made weapon between his teeth.

"Well, what do we have here, another freak'n kid?" A large patchy and dirty, leathery face spits a clump of mucus onto the ground by Destin's foot. "Where's the rest of ya?" The tall heavyset man pulls Destin close until their noses nearly touch.

"I, I, I'm the only one! It's just me! Please, don't, don't kill me!" Destin begs for his life with the steel between his lips. Scared, intrigued and caught off guard by the presence of another human, the boy looks up at the man. "Wait, who are you? Where... where do you come..." Destin's stutter is interrupted by the impact of the gun, as it is yanked from his mouth and slapped across the back of his head. "Stop, that hurts! Maybe I can help you, just, just tell me what you want!" Blood trickles down his neck. Destin pleads before a kick to the chest sends his small, thin body sliding backwards in the sand.

"Names are no good to a dead person. But, since you asked, I'm Proctor, and you are... the only one? Blah, that's what they all say." The large man seemingly peers into the fear in his soul. "It was men like your fathers and their seeds who destroyed this world. It was the children who squandered everything we had... and stood for. And thanks to men like me, it will never happen again, mate. I Proctor, will fix everything in this world. There is a new god here today, boy." The tall, dark figure knocks the dust from his old cowboy hat and tilts it upon his head as a bright light flashes across his face; skin and blood fly. He is shot in the right eye by a flare gun from afar. Destin pushes away his arm and kicks the man square in the center of the knee cap. Letting off a round into the air from his hand held cannon, blindly, the giants body crashes to the ground in agony.

A short silhouette stood in the distance behind Destin as he overhears the voices of more men approaching around the building. Deciding to follow the one who saved him, the boy quickly grabs his bag from the ground and rushes out to the shadowy figure. The stranger directs him with the hand gestures of a fingerless glove. Destin runs off, trailing the person to the safety confines between two large pillars of sand and broken stone. Crawling in a hole, inside some sort of metal structure once used for storage and random shelter, Destin plops down on a legless, torn, stained sofa, just across from the stranger wrapped in light layers of rags and cloth. Rubbing his throbbing head, Destin feels the wetness of the blood on his fingertips and gazes at the dark figure. He watches the stranger slide a metal panel over the bright entrance, turning the already dark space, pitch black. Inside the darkness, Destin shoves his hand into the large pocket of his pants; pulling out a small waxy object. "Hey... look, I don't require anything. I just want to say thanks for saving me out there. I... I can't believe it. It's like a dream. Sorry, but I haven't seen other people in a long time. Seems like I'm the only one living sometimes." Destin lights a small piece of candle, a row of old electric heaters and small generators come into view.

"And I'm, I'm happy to see you as well, my friend." Finally speaking, the stranger removes a wrap of cloth from around his head and face revealing a brown haired, Caucasian male in his twenties. Entranced with Destin's dark skin, he grins, face expressing enthusiasm towards conversation. "And... you're welcome." A calm and even more mellowed voice mutters out next. "Even though there are not many of us, we still have to be careful. There are still dangers out there, ya know?"

"My name is Destin." The boy holds out his hand. "I'm a Scav." [Scav's are what was referred to as scavengers at the time]

"Tyler, nice to meet another." The young man greets, leaning forward, he connects with a hearty handshake. "You didn't see them coming out there? I could hear them a mile away."

"No, I didn't see hear them at all in the sand storm. That

man… who were those people back there?" Destin tucks his arms into pockets along his upper clothing for warmth.

"Hunters. They're a people from our parent's time who blame their own for wiping out the old ways, and causing all of this. By killing every parent and their offspring's alike, the Hunters believe that a new world could exist… even better than the old. Just of them." Tyler opens a label-less can of old beans and eats the foul smelling mush with two fingers. "But from what I've seen, they're extremely dumb. They even kill each other over petty rivals. I would know, I've been around them a long time now. I like to keep my eyes on them, where ever they move. They can cause a lot of trouble if you don't see them coming. Over time, I bet they'll wipe themselves out, I guarantee it. They're pretty messy. They're worse than rats."

"How many hunters are out there? Have you seen any more people around… you know, Scav's like us?" Destin questions, Tyler tosses him a blanket and provides more light by igniting a wick upon a lid of animal fat. "Where do you come from?"

"Get some rest my friend, you're going to need it. We can't stay here talking, forever." Tyler stretches out on an old pile of paper, blankets and clothes, gathered from around the wasteland. "It must be a sign that you decided to drop in, I was leaving this place today." He sits the can down on the floor. "You're like a regular angel. It gave me hope when I saw you."

"Hope? Are there any others like us?" Destin asks again, this time sitting upright in a more serious posture. He takes a very small nibble from an old half eaten candy bar in his pocket.

"You mean survivors?"

"Yeah."

"No one knows for sure how many Scavengers are out there my friend. Let's just hope that if there are, they're not like those Hunter fellows!" Tyler laughs, "But your my first in a long while. Can't really give the other Scav's I've seen much credit. The Hunters always kill them on sight." Pulling a blanket of animal hide over his body; Tyler drapes a flap of paper over his dirty face. "You sure ask a lot of questions for a person just meeting someone. I'll turn on the heaters when those Hunters have gone a bit further away. They create a bit of a racket when you turn them on. I got a few stashed around, never know when you'll need one." Peeking from under the folds of paper, Tyler eyes Destin taking interest in a small leather book he dropped on the floor. "That book right there... is special." Tyler sits up and scoops the book in his hand. "I found this. Inside is history, important things to know. It's the stories of the last people who found it. You know, travelers who could write, Scav's, people just like you and me, some good and some bad? Heck, I even started adding my own stories to it. As long as I have it, I know there's always hope in finding people." Tyler tucks it away somewhere beneath the animal hide.

Resting his head on the arm of the sofa, Destin rolls on his back and props his legs upon the other end. Not knowing what else to say, and having not been in one on one contact with another person in years, Destin silently watches Tyler fall asleep. Thinking of the Hunters, what other people could possibly be like and what the future may hold, he shoos away a small, sickly fly and stare at the small clouds of heat puffing from his nose and mouth. Tonight was the first night of nightfall in three days. Turning to his candle which eventually goes out, Destin watches the small wick upon Tyler's homemade candle, until it too, dies out completely.

Sand blows inside the burrow of the temporary shelter through its now open entrance, filling the cubical shelter. Destin emerges from a pool of sand that nearly buries the sofa, choking and gagging. Pausing still, he listens for any sound of movement. Daylight shine in from outside, illuminating the space. "Tyler? Tyler!" Destin calls out in a low voice. Crawling out from a small sand dune, Destin lowers his sun specs from the top of his head down to his eyes. He sees no signs of life as normal. A strong wind continuously blow across the landscape as Destin journeys out into the dunes across unsettling dips in the sand. Scattered pieces of wood, cloth and material point to a small, foreign object half covered in the dirt. Walking to the item, Destin picks it up, identifying it as the small leather book Tyler was carrying. Hoping Tyler was okay, Destin senses something bad in the air, places the book inside the inner lining of his clothes and continues on his way to nowhere. The brief interaction with Tyler, the stranger was a memorable one and soon, being alone again made even the experience with even the Hunter a bit missed.

Days become weeks, weeks become months, and soon years has passed. Traveling in the desert ruins, hot sand and jagged, burning rocks rip at Destin's clothes and wear holes in the cloth and dry hay that wrapped his feet. Crossing paths with the skeletal remains of a person who perhaps died of hunger, Destin respectfully take the shoes of the dead in exchange for a stranger's eulogy and a poor man's burial. Taking time to neatly cover the bones with stones, dirt and sand, he recites a short, yet decent prayer. Occasionally making time to read from the tablet Tyler carried, Destin becomes fascinated by the encounters of people who lost the book. Learning how to read from his parents who were tortured and killed when he was a young, Destin read the book from the beginning up to its last entry that lasted until he reached the end of the desert, which didn't go on forever as he thought. Learning of life during earlier times through pictures and various entries, Destin learns of plants and various ways to make fire. With nothing else to read, Destin closes the book and incorporates the knowledge in his future exploits. Entertained by a new terrain of plants and unbelievable vegetation; he collects rocks, herbs and leaves while exploring a jungle of never seen before wilderness.

The world in which Destin thought was dying and depleted, appear to be nonexistent in this region. Flourishing and very much alive; the remains of man's rapidly growing technological world had died, and was replaced by what was now pure, untamed and raw nature. Haven't ever recalled hearing or seeing such a variety of animals alive except for lizards, snakes and a few hungry rodents, Destin found himself engaged in a parade of frightening new sounds and creatures. Here, Destin saw the creation of GOD which was merely the outcome of man's wars and how it did indeed set them on a path of extinction. Yet the natural beauty from where Destin sat, even made him question if the devastation and collapse of man was even worth rebuilding. The area was so lush and beautiful, Destin could hold the memory of it in his mind forever. "No more factors, no more streets, no more animals at our feet." Destin recalls an old childhood song. He closes the leather tablet and puts it away, envisioning how life might have been before the great wars and sickness came. In a once, suburban neighborhood, bombed, destroyed, now overtaken by grass, trees and vines, Destin soaks his feet in a flooded, sunken road that formed a cool creek of waddling ducks and bugs. In his thoughts, Destin stare at the reflection of the clear sky over his shoulders in the water; the ripples he make, seem to chase the birds above him out of his field of vision. Dipping his hand and pulling it out, droplets of water from a small facial towel in his hand, fall, making small, exploding waves. Looking closely, something he has only heard tales about wiggled beneath the light current. Thought long ago dead and wiped out from man's toxic pollution, a fish, a fist sized salmon to be exact, swam calmly upstream beneath his feet. Searching for something to kill it with, Destin stops in place. Although hungry, he is reminded by the fish, the odds of his own survival. Life was already hard without things trying to kill you; Destin thought of the Hunters. Feeling sympathy, Destin lets the fish live. Wiping filth from his face, Destin's stomach growls loudly, convincing him to venture out to forage. Food was always needed and finding a secure shelter to rest and hide was always the priority for the day. Astounded by the rare deliciously colored insects, plants and new animals he saw, Destin perches on the edge of an old building, looking down into a valley of a crumbled city. Taking out some old chips from his bag, he glances down at a reflection of himself on the side of a shiny pipe. Laughing at the hair on his face and how old he's gotten, Destin suddenly wonders about the number of people who could actually still exist in the world. Suddenly a faint scream catches his attention, and as if a he dreamt it, it ceases to be heard for several minutes. Another scream, totally different in pitch and tone echoes from the center of the crumbling city. Excited, Destin stops wearily and remembers the violet man he came across years ago. This time, finding a long and sturdy piece of log, he wields it as a weapon and rushes off towards the sounds of the person. Through the tall grass and weeds, the young man runs cautiously through the thickets of thorny plants that slice at his clothes and skin. Between toppled cars and areas totally covered in nature and vines, he jumps and slides down a tilted telephone pole to a strip of broken road. Trying to catch the sight of anyone still on the premises, Destin hurries over jagged and sharp stone and glass material from fallen buildings; glass and metal jab brutally into his worn, thin soled shoes.

Suddenly, seeing movement in the brush; Destin's dark brown oval eyes make contact with something fierce. Heart pounding, adrenaline replacing happy emotions; Destin freezes with fear. A cold sweat breaks over Destin's body, he trembles; legs instantly giving into weakness at the startling sight that crept before him. Directly ahead, lurking in front of him, a survivor of something ancient, something that Destin could have only fathomed from the deepest depths of a nightmarish dream, growled. The first eye full of a set of two inch long teeth drops Destin's heart to his stomach as the sheer half a ton weight of the great beast that faced him, cringed his soul. A creature, not known in this time, but created through experimentation long ago in the twentieth century, steals Destin's breath away with a cold and powerful stare of its huge yellow eyes. In heavy pants of bass, a Liger (A Lion mixed and bred with a Tiger) licks its huge mouth of twitching white whiskers, and snarls agitatedly, before releasing a ferocious roar. Mainly a dusty orange, large white patches and black stripes colored the giants powerful four legs and muscular upper body. Clearly illustrating its dominant rank over man and other primitive life forms, the Liger sinks low and still inside the canvas of concrete and forestry. Large ears of the beast arch attentively back, then forward in Destin's direction, directly sending a warning to him.

Snapping out of his scare, Destin jolts onto the low rooftop of a sunken building. Running, he could hear the Liger pouncing after him. Quickly catching up to Destin, the large cat swings its solid, muscular arm, slicing through his bag. As shingles from the rooftop slide beneath his feet, Destin feels part of the creatures razor sharp claws sink into his back. With great force, Destin is spun off the rooftop into the thickets below. Losing his weapon, Destin crashes to the ground of rocks and weeds. Rolling over, Destin lifts his head and spots his weapon, a branch of wood shaped like a spear, at least six feet away in the grass. Raising up, he pushes his tired and bruised body forward to retrieve the spear; but is thrown back against the dirt by the ferocious roar of the giant feline. Landing directly in front of him, the Liger steps on the tip of Destin's spear with its massive paw. Howling at the Sun, oddly, the large animal begin to scratch and thrash about the ground. Then kicking and bellowing, the big cat snorts, swiping at its nose as if it was having a hard time breathing. Gagging, the cat leaps at Destin eagerly. Crashing at his feet, the liger chokes, life force quickly departing from the cats body as it reaches out, touching the tip of Destin's foot. "What?" Destin stoops down to examine the beast. Almost like liquid, a strange dark substance flow over the concrete just below the Liger as a texture of blackness envelopes and blankets over its head, body and beautiful fur. The odd darkness pour over the beast into a now, growing pool around the feline's body. Feeling a tickling sensation of coolness, streaming over his own hands and legs, followed by pinching, Destin gazes down. Lifting one hand, he realizes the damp feel wasn't liquid at all. Face turning pale and the hairs on his arms and neck standing on ends, Destin stomp and shakes his clothes free of millions upon millions of ants that begin to cover him from the ground. "Oh, what is this? Get off!" Destin dances about in a frenzy, having never to encounter attacking ants before.

"Ryelle!" A voice shouts out as Destin spots a woman of African American decent climbing a bus with something in her arms. Next to a car pile, desperately trying to escape the hungry ants, the woman climbs a vehicle that stood upright on its nose with a child.

"Wait, hey!" Leaving the Liger, Destin follows the two people. "Wait!" Traveling much lighter, he notices the large rip in his bag. Missing most of his supplies, Destin still manages to find a can of aerosol spray. "Hold on!" Destin yells to the woman. Knocking insects from his arms and body, he ran for the ocean of ants surrounding the bus. "I can help you!"

The higher the woman climbed with the child, the taller the ants built their ladders of connecting bodies to reach them. Covering the whole nose of the flipped bus, the ants, unified in numerous colonies, gather and share data and information with great precision and accuracy. It was no surprise that the ants too had secretly dominated and strategically colonized the world. Highly intelligent, the ants began to skillfully block off each side of the bus to get to the woman.

"I need fire. Do you have fire, a fire maker?" Destin, hopping around, searches his bag and pockets for a lighter or matches. "Where is it?" He mutters. "I can help you! I think."

"Wha… what? Help us?" The woman screams, beating off ants from her legs with one hand.

"Yes, I can help you, but I need something that makes fire!" Destin jumps about, keeping clear of the multiplying, mountains of attacking insects. Fidgeting uncontrollably, he receives a multitude of tiny, stinging bites. Stepping off balanced, Destin sees a grim figure burst through a mound of ants,

"Zenna…" Covered in blood, swollen bites and hanging skin, something resembling a man reaches out for Destin. A tidal wave of ants flood and fill the sockets of the man's eyes and mouth, suffocating his esophagus.

Eyes and skin eaten, the man leaps out; Destin jumps back in fright, kicking him backwards into the sea of ants as the woman tosses a lighter near. Misjudging the distance, the woman watches the lighter drown in the whirlpool of swarming ants. Screaming, the woman frantically dust off the scared child, realizing her pants legs were covered again. Enveloped with crawling insects from head to toe; except for his mouth, Destin is convinced there is only one chance to survive. Tightening his lips, he runs off at full speed; layers of ants topple off into the wind from his body. In a single bound, Destin leaps and dives into the river of ants where the lighter landed. A spark ignites in front of the bus, deep beneath the body of moving insects. Waves of ants ignite into fire as their bodies explode in every direction. Their small, frail bodies break away from the towering ladders in a scatter of free falling flames and ashes. The walls of ants shatter around Destin as he rises from the falling bodies of burning insects holding a lighter against the spray of his aerosol can until it ran out. Spitting, he pat's out the small fires from his clothes inside the snow of drifting, black floating carcasses of burned ants. "That was incredible." Destin shakes the rest from his rags and looks on top of the bus at the woman and child who were still killing off ants. "Are you two okay?" He then glances at miles and miles of land littered with ants. Tossing down the can, he whips out another unknown can of aerosol spray. Keeping the nearest insects at bay, Destin stares down closely near his feet, noticing that the ground was also littered with skeletal remains. "Uhhh… I don't think it's safe for you to stay up there. I see why there are so many bugs here. We're standing on their food bed! I don't know how much longer you have but… maybe you should hurry?"

Climbing down first, a small dark haired boy shook out his clothes and stomps the ground at the ants that crackled beneath their feet. Of a tan tint, with wide slanting eyes, the boy smiles and steps to the side shyly. Next, the woman, with thick coarse hair, brown skin, and fresh holes torn in her clothing from her journey climbs down. Rugged and heavy black boots cover the woman's feet as sections of her hair matted into dreads. Beautiful dark eyes complimented a full set of dark brows and lips that spoke the words of gratitude. "Thank you, thank you for saving us." She smacks at her arms and shakes the remaining ants out her head. "We should go, now." She glimpse over at the little boy.

"This way." Destin nods and directs them to a hillside he passed on the way there. The hike up the steep slope provides an opportunity for them to speak as they reach enough distance away to finally slow down and catch a breath.

"I am Zenna, and this… is Ryelle. I'm from the Eastland's, the only one from my tribe who is still living. The woman places an arm around the boy and strokes his jet black hair.

"And he, where is he from? Brave little tike, haven't seen a real child since I was a child. They're amazing! They're like real little people!" Destin kneels to get a closer view of the boy.

"I… I don't know… where he's from. He doesn't talk much." Zenna, hesitant to talk, displays a small, Mexican kid with a full round face under her arm. Looking Destin in the eyes, Zenna felt as though she could trust him and decides it was okay to open up to him, "I, I found him trapped in an old destroyed… place. We've been together ever since. There was another who traveled with us but… back there." Sadly, Zenna's eyes water over the loss life of the man. "He was our only friend and a good person." Her eyes trickled with tears, she holds back her pain and catches a falling leaf in her hand. Starting to crumple it, Zenna releases the leaf and continues walking. She looks back at Destin who was having a hard time getting up. "You're hurt. Wait, let me help you." Zenna notices blood on the back of Destin's clothing. "Quickly, take off your top garments." She rips off the bottom half of her top. "Something got you good, what did this?"

"Some beast in the wilderness back there, right before I found you."

"You must be careful in the wilds, it can hold many dangers." Zenna wraps the large and deep scratches on his back with the ripped cloth. "What about you, what's your name? Where are you from?" She helps Destin put his clothes back on.

"Thanks, the names Destin." He stands. "I don't really remember exactly where I'm from. I was too young to remember. All I do know is it was all destroyed by some type of blast, and fire…. lots of it. It killed everybody except…" Destin quiets and lowers his head. Turning, Destin gazes off into the distance and changes the subject. "Where you two headed?"

"North, I hear people are there, traders, and a colony. What about you, where were you going?" Continuing walking, Zenna pulls her hair back, plucks a fig from a bush they pass and eats it.

"Nowhere specific, just decided to see what else is out there, living off the land. I'm from the sands; first time I've seen green-land. This is the farthest I've ever made it." Destin smiles, "Yesterday, I was alone, I thought the world was made out of sand, today I'm walking through plants with people. Day to day is how I see it, it's always lucky to see tomorrow. Tomorrow seems to always bring something new." Destin grins, happy just to have someone else to talk too, to be in the presence of a real female and a child was a extra bonus to his life. Never had he remembered seeing one of such. So lively, yet reserved, Zenna made him feel a strange way inside when he looked at her. Unlike the pictures of women in the filthy literature or centuries old ads he came across, she was very real, and reminded him of someone whom he hadn't seen in a very long time since he was a small boy. That soothing tone in her voice, the way she warmly interacted with the mute child, the way she looked at him with hope and compassion; she reminded Destin… of his mother.

"Why don't you come with us? We could use the company and by the looks of it, so could you." Zenna offers.

"To the north, I dunno? Do you really think there's a colony there, a real colony… with people?" Destin debates the offer inside his mind.

"Yes, and even if there isn't, I think it's worth a look see, don't you think?" Zenna smiles back, slinging a small sack over her neck and shoulders. "I've met and talked to people… that's where most of them are heading. To the Northlands."

"You've talked to people? Others like us? What were they like? I hope they weren't Hunters." Destin checks the hole sliced in his bag.

"Hunters? Never heard of them and I haven't met any in these parts. Who are they?" Zenna ask, curiously watches the ants still on their trail, carry away his spilled goods in the distance.

"I haven't seen them much and only encountered them once in my life time. They're people like us, well… wild men who kill people like us and kids. I met a guy who taught me about them. He told me not to hang around too long when you see them. Maybe you've come across him? His name was Tyler, I'll never forget him." Destin stretches his hand inside the hole of the bag, analyzing how bad the damage was.

"No, sorry, don't recall meeting anyone by a name like that. Hey, don't look so sad." Zenna looks at Destin's troubled face. "I can fix your sack. Here, let me see it." She examines the hole as they exit a patch of forest, entering the streets of the old city. Traveling slow with child, cautiously, keeping an eye out for dangers, Destin and Zenna walk along the concrete sidewalks that bleed into the grassy earth between a strip of crumbling buildings and a broken tar roads. Passing the rusted frames of ancient vehicles, long ago forgotten, the two cut through a large parking lot into a park, overran with an overgrowth of weeds and foliage. Exchanging stories and ideology, the young man and woman began to connect and learn about each other.

"I can't believe you think people actually built all of these structures." Destin stops to draw pictures of the things around him inside the small leather book he kept. "How come out of all the people you claim to have seen, no one is doing it now?"

"I'm telling you, we were inventors in the beginning, we ruled over the machines. We, gave them life." Zenna peers over a valley of fallen planes and helicopters. "Man created the metal birds which flew us anywhere we wanted to go, even up there." She points to stars that could be still seen in the darkening, day sky.

"No way, I refuse to believe it. It had to be GOD, or a highly advanced race from the stars. Have you seen the giant green lady with the broken sword?" Destin refers to what was once known as the statue of liberty.

"Oh yes, in many old papers left from the time before, but never with my own eyes."

"Well, whomever built her, they had to be giants as well." suggest Destin.

"I would love to have seen the green woman, she sounds powerful." Zenna eyes Ryelle chasing away lighting bugs that began to pop up around them.

"I was told, GOD gave her a sword of fire. The green lady, angered by the wicked hearts of man below, stuck her sword into the great waters that surrounded the terrible city which man lived. And from her blow came the great sands, my home. An elder told me this when I was young, his father, saw this with his own eyes." Destin stoops down, picks up a rock and tosses it into the opening.

"This GOD of yours, how do you know he existed? How do you know he did all these things you say?"

"Have you ever had a Twinkie?"

"What's a Twinkie?" Zenna and the little boy laughs. "That's a funny word."

"It's not funny. Its food, a sweet loaf that comes in a really small package. It gives you energy and happiness whenever you eat it. It's the food of the CREATOR. GOD left it behind for man, it never goes rotten and never spoils. Our fathers, father and their fathers, father, use to have them all the time. It is why they lived so long. If you ever find one, it's a really delicious treat! GOD created it, and it still exist today."

"Have you ever found one of these...Twinkies?" Zenna ask curiously.

"Yes, twice."

"Luck has been with you I see." Slyly grinning, Zenna walks onward beside him.

Long vines extend endlessly to the rooftops of gutted out buildings still standing throughout the elements of the harsh years as grass and wild bushes push up through cracks and sewers along the old and broken, concrete block, sidewalks. Remains of the past lay buried beneath untamed, yet colorful blossoming trees, while snakes of unbelievable sizes, slither secretly between its natural beauty for cover. Destin swat away an array of bugs flying and scurrying about, spotting and old house in a canopy of forest. A nest of large spider's guard a wooden door of the old, boarded up house missing windows, which still remained barely standing in the woods. Snapped tree branches are tossed out the way. A complex weave of webbing is lit with fire that spread to the large and plump spider eggs that occupied it. The front door of the home is kicked off its hinges as the last surviving spider finds a way to bite gentle holes into its eggs, releasing hundreds of their offspring out into free world.

"This looks like a good place to rest for now. Ryelle, when I lift this up, fasten that chair on the door like we showed you." Zenna instructs the small boy. He drags over a chair, leans and shoves its back under the doorknob just as she says.

"Hello, is anyone in here?" Destin always yells when entering a large, newly discovered building, never to receive a response in return. In an elegantly decorated dusty living room, Destin heads up a set of stairs to the next floor. He stares at Zenna's thin frame going into another room, which appeared to be a kitchen. Up the dirt covered staircase, Destin bats away more cobwebs, winding up in a large hall of connecting bedrooms. Peeping into what look like a child's room, he leaves it untouched and moves to the next room. Looking around, he thinks of how life might have been before global warming and the wars. Standing by the master bedroom, he moves in front of another room, apparently a teenagers. Destin glances at the dusty piles of clothes and old peeling posters of funny dressed people wielding weird objects, known at one time as instruments. "Wow, what a waste." Destin rambles through the clothes and dresser drawers before walking back downstairs. Finding nothing good to salvage, he quickly leaves the room; running smack into Zenna. They head-butt, Destin bust his lip against Zennas teeth.

"Oow, are you okay? That's a heck of a way to kiss someone. You nearly knocked out my teeth, Destin! That hurts!" Zenna holds her mouth as Destin sucks his bleeding bottom lip.

"My apologies, Zen, I didn't see you. You turned the corner so fast." Destin hears a slight unfamiliar sound beside them. "What is that, Ryelle, is… he laughing?" He and Zenna both glance down at Ryelle, who covers his mouth with both hands, tickled by their mishaps.

"I haven't heard him laugh that hard in ages. I believe he finds our misfortunes quite funny." Zenna places her hands on her waist.

"Is that so? Is that his problem? He doesn't laugh much, humph? Looks like we'll just have to do something about that now wont we?" Destin looks at Zenna, Zenna looks at Destin. They both give chase after the child, tickling him to the floor of the house.

As the day went onward, the three easily get more acquainted by gathering food together from the woods and around the city. Collecting water, edible flowers and berries, they find themselves having a picnic and keeping each other entertained by trying on different clothes from the house. Bonding, Destin, Zenna and Ryelle roam by day and share shelter by night, becoming more and more like a small family as the days progressed. The three slowly continue northward as the days again turn into weeks, and weeks into months once more. Coming to dead ends, cliffs, dried up riverbeds and unpassable bridges, Destin, Zenna and the boy change directions dozens of times over. Discovering new barren towns, nearly erased and blown to shambles, temporarily, Destin settle inside another abandoned house for several days. Around another property barely standing; wild horses run freely upon green acres as the three travelers turn in for another night.

Dreaming of another time and place where people of different colors lived and rode on machines with wheels, Destin could see Zenna and Ryelle running for him as they cheered and played in a beautiful garden. Tyler appears out of nowhere and joins them happily in laughter. Joining hands, they make a ring. As their smiles spun in a circle around him, Destin could see Tyler pointing at the small leather book that hung from twine around his neck. Slowing down, Destin felt the inside his garments, realizing that he no longer had the book in his possession. Lifting his head, Destin looks at Zenna puzzled; her happy expression is replaced by sadness and an utter look of confusion. As the three stop spinning around him, Destin peers down at a freshly made, large, open wound inside her chest; Zenna's blood sprays into his mouth and across his face. A Hunter stands behind her falling body, holding a smoking gun.

"Destin wake up! Did you hear that?" Dripping blood, Zenna peers up at Destin from the ground. "Destin!" Destin feels a strong push and awakens from dreaming to the sound of Zenna's voice over him. "I hear something!"

"What's this… what's wrong with him?" Destin replies, still groggy from sleeping. He tries to quickly remember what he was dreaming about, with no such success. "Oh, Zenna."

"Destin, I heard a noise coming from downstairs!" Zenna grabs Ryelle who was asleep between them and pulls him closer.

Quickly sitting upright, Destin hears the noise for himself. "Stay here, I'll take a look. If I'm not back soon, run, take Ryelle and hide." He whispers, frightening Zenna even more. "I'll yell at the tops of my lungs if there's a threat, okay?"

"Okay." Zenna nods, her eyes fill with worry. "Destin..." She sits up and places a soft warm hand on his face. "be careful." She plants an unforgettable kiss on his lips as he leaves the bedroom of their temporary settlement.

First checking the bedrooms and bath upstairs, Destin sees nothing out of the ordinary. Breaking off the shower curtain rod from the wall, he uses the metal pole as a weapon. Gripping it tightly, Destin slowly creeps downstairs clutching the rod in both hands like a baseball bat. "Is there someone down there?" Into a huge dining area already a mess, he finds the room completely turned upside down in old, broken furniture and miscellaneous things, scattered about everywhere. "Who could have done this?" He thinks to himself. "Who's here?" Destin asks loudly; the sound of an empty bottle clings against the floor. The back of someone's coat moves behind a bar separating the kitchen from the dining area. Raising the pole high above his head in the clobbering position, Destin inches to the kitchen. Having found boxes of pasta and rice, the sound of continuous eating and the raiding of cabinet's disrespects him. Angered, Destin announces his presence once more before attacking. "I know what you're doing, I can hear you eating! Please, stop... eating our food!" Destin builds the nerves to be aggressive. "You've found food have you? Well, in this place... we share! So... come on out, show yourself or... I, I'm coming in to get you!" Destin yells as the intruder continues on with what it was doing. Mad, Destin listens to the sounds of heavy breathing with the weapon in hand. Ready to defend Zenna and Ryelle upstairs; Destin, gathering the courage needed, charges into the kitchen screaming. A large brown grizzly bear rises six feet over him. A tremendous roar rattle the windows and rumble through every wall inside the house; the bear unarms Destin with one swing of its mighty paw. The very tips of the other claw quickly shred cloth and meat from Destin's chest; his body is flown backwards into Zenna's arms. She screams, her scent reminds Destin of the pleasurable aroma of honeysuckles he smelled in the mornings inside the forest. Dying in her presence wasn't such a bad ideal, Destin thought. Ryelle dashes out in front of them, bravely. He holds a bottle of aerosol spray up to a lighter just as he remembered seeing Destin do.

Lurching forward and jumping backwards, the grizzly dodges the hot burst of flames directed by the child. Pressing upon the button of the can, steadily flicking the lighter, Ryelle's facial expression falls blank as no more fire emits from the can. As the can is emptied, only the aroma of a hot, perfume scent saturates the air. Growling and snarling, showing solely nothing but teeth, the bear snaps forward, a bright flash and a loud bang breaks the attack. The large grizzly collapse to the floor seeping blood from a hole in the side of its neck. Still moving, a second gunshot fires into the animal. Dragging its large body, the bear claws the floor to get to Destin and Zenna; a hole is blown into the animals head, dropping it permanently. The bear takes its last breath as the tall silhouette of a man dressed in a long tattered jacket stand behind it, pointing a gun at the three travelers.

"Who are you, Raiders, Scavs? What the hell are you doing in my shelter? Leave now!" Illuminated by nearby lit candles, a grumpy, wrinkled face threatens in a gruff voice.

"Please, we're just heading north. We needed shelter for the night!" Zenna pleads; the old man, with a long holed robe underneath his jacket, walks over and holds the barrel of the gun to her nose.

"For the night? Ha, looks like you all been here for a while!" Missing teeth, the stranger peers around the shadows of the room with his mouth hanging open. "I don't take kindly to people defiling my bed and home. "Peasants." He spits on the floor. "I should have left you to the jaws of that filthy varmint!"

"Please, we, we mean you no harm! We'll leave, but right now my friend needs help. That thing just clawed him badly. Please, can you help him? We'll leave but… I'm not leaving without him! I'll do anything you ask, just please… can you help us?" Zenna begs, the man eyes sparkle with lust and sinful temptations.

As the wheels inside older man's complex mind churn with thoughts and ideas, his dry cracked lips curl into a sinister grin. His blue pupil eyes outlined in gray, water. How long it had been since he too had seen or felt the touch of a warm woman. And it was in that instance, with the gun held firmly in place to her face, that Zenna knew that she too, reminded the old man of someone close, perhaps a daughter or a mistress.

Quickly losing blood, Destin passes out under Zenna's beautiful face. Feeling her tight grip loosen and hands slip from around him, he falls unconscious. Awakening on some kind of wooden vehicle pulled by horses, Destin sits up stiff and sore. Covered in a warm pile of dirty, lent ball filled blankets, Destin's eyes gain focus. He stares at the back of a large head steering a well preserved carriage from days past, just like the ones he saw in old magazines. The big head becomes the back of the gray headed old man, who was sitting next to Zenna. Destin feels a light gently touch upon his shoulder; Ryelle smiles next to him.

"Good morning Destin, I'm glad you woke up. You okay?" Ryelle spoke soft and timidly.

"Yes, I guess." Destin tries to move; surprised by the child's voice. "You… talk?" A sharp pain whips across his midsection. Lifting clothing and linen, he reveals rows of finely woven stitches across his chest and stomach. Touching his skin, he plucks tiny leaves from a green herbal mesh packed into his wounds.

"Destin! Stop that! You know how hard supplies are to come by? Take it easy, that animal nearly scratched you to death! We're safe for the moment." Zenna smiles looking back at Destin from over her seat, she blows a kiss and winks. "This is Avious, the one who help you. He's going to take us all the way North." Zenna turns back around and glances over at the man.

"Thankyou." Destin lowers his shirt and falls back, dealing with the pain. Hardly able to believe that they were being driven by wild animals, he stares, amazed at the sight, smell and fact that he was up close and personal with real live creatures he had never seen before; horses. Sharing a piece of snake with Ryelle from a large bag, Destin begins to question how Zenna knew which way was north, when the north-star they were following didn't shine during the day. Never having to trust anyone with his life, Destin becomes slightly paranoid. Sensing bad vibes in the air, Destin makes brief eye contact with Avious inside a rearview mirror attached to the side of the carriage by rope and nails. "How long was I out?" He glimpse into the man's dark, crow's feet, riddled, eyes.

"Oh, nearly a day or so. I had to use tranquilizers so you wouldn't feel the pain. Guess I used a little too much. You're healing good; the herbs are working well." Avious cut his eyes back to the road.

"Yeah, we would have been beast food if it wasn't for Avious, he saved our life. We we're in his home, can you believe that? All that time we thought we were alone... funny isn't it?" Zenna stare at the weird vines and plants covering parts of roads and crumbling statues they pass.

"I suppose, I'm just grateful to still be alive." States Destin; Ryelle offers him a pear.

"There's a safe place a few hours from here, we'll rest there for the night. We have to be careful, you just can't sleep anywhere, you know? Look around us, nature has taken back what is rightfully hers. Our world is wild now, full of predator and even greater dangers. Stay with me, and you'll live." Avious pats Zenna on the leg and eyes Destin's reflection coldly before returning his focus to the terrain at hand. Destin receives an odd feeling in his gut about the man. He looks down at the weird shaped fruit Ryelle gave him.

Riding longer than expected, off road, over hillsides, back down into the old town, the carriage comes to an old shack constructed of metal, tin and eroded ply wood. The wind whistles chilly against the cluster of limber tress that bump and lean against the frame of the tattered shack. With no signs of any activity, still, the night brought about a surprising symphony of frogs and chirping crickets, which brought a desolate, reassuring peace to the howling valleys in the distance. With the small child, Ryelle, resting within the confines of the shack, the three adults sit around a small fire pit in front.

"It'll be about a few week's travel to reach the north, but we'll get there." Avious reassures them, chewing on a twig of straw, he roast four small pieces of meaty game on a slender stick by fire. "Sure you don't want any, they're pretty hearty?" He offers; Destin and Zenna look at the long scaly and rodent like tails attached to the partially cooked critters, then at the set of monstrous teeth that aligned the mouths of the tiny, alien looking heads. Having mainly eaten age old, canned food, insects, plants, and an occasional poisoned snake from time to time, Destin and Zenna's noses turn and stomachs feel queasy at the smell of the roasting meat. "Well suit yourself." Avious get up to lead the horses to the nearby stream, first fetching extra blankets and clothing for them to lay on. Returning with the bedding materials, Avious walks off in the darkness toward the sound of the horses. "I'll keep first watch, then you two… keep your ears open for the usual worries."

On his back, Destin gazes up at the black sky. "Zenna, how much do you trust this fellow? I mean… I'm not questioning your judgment but, I've been on my own most of my life and out of the few people that I've encountered, most just do mainly for themselves." He whispers.

"Destin… he's gotten us this far in a matter of days and he saved you. It would have taken us seasons to make it this far on our own. That must count for something?" Zenna kisses him on the forehead and pulls some large old rags over his body.

"Yes but… I dunno, guess I still have fears of that man I came across. Guess we have to do what we have to do?" Destin picks up a stick of burnt squirrel. "Maybe it is best we stick together."

"Do you trust me?" Zenna scoots closer to him, gazing at the side of his face, at his jaw line, strong and pronounced. She had never seen a man's skin as smooth as hers, but Destin was young.

Hungry, Destin build the nerves to take a bite from the hot rodent; he takes a hard swallow, sits the squirrel shish-kabob by the fire untouched, and lays his head back. "I suppose." He responds to Zenna. A twinkle of light catches Destin's eye, he notices the north-star gleaming high in the clear sky, but in the opposite direction they were heading. Destin looks over at Zenna who automatically climbs over him. Her hair smelled of honey and cones and body of the sweetest scented pollens, making his heart beat uncontrollably fast and awkward.

"Trust me." Zenna gently kisses him on the neck, and works her way up to his chin. "I care for you Destin." Her soft full brown lips presses against his. Pulling up a blanket of sewn animal pelts over their bodies, Zenna, runs her warm hands along the sides of his injured chest, warming something inside him.

"Before you, my life… had no meaning. But now, I'm starting to feel like maybe there's a greater reason for me to be here, a purpose to survive." Destin squeezes her gently. "I… I care for you a great deal as well, Zenna." He looks back at her nervously as her face draws in closer to his. "I've never felt this way before," She becomes a blur as two soft lips push into his. Slowly caressing her, a sudden burst of emotions lead Destin into a discreet and passionate bout of love making under the moon. And as their heartbeats create new rhythms of heated intensity into the hours ahead, eventually, both fall victim to slumber, secure and cuddled in the arms of the other, until the next morning.

Jumping up to the sounds of rustling bushes and rattling tin buckets, Destin and Zenna arise to the sight of Avious running through the tall grass towards them.

"Get up and go! They're here, they're coming!" Avious shouts at the top of his lungs while snatching gear from around the camp.

"What's happening? Ryelle, Ryelle!" Zenna hurries inside the shack and pulls the seven year old child to his feet.

"What's going on? Who's coming?" Destin quickly puts on his clothes and thinks.

"Hunters, Raiders, bandits, whatever you want to call them, boy! If you want to live, better get to the horses!" Avious points to the woods as they run to the carriage behind Zenna and the boy. "You drive!"

"I drive? Drive, what, me? But I don't know how to! I only…" Destin tries to explain; Avious cuts him off.

"Drive!" Avious shouts leaping onto the back of the carriage backwards, aiming his rifle.

Destin quickly lifts Ryelle up to Zenna, tearing a few stitches, then climbs aboard behind him. Imitating what he watched Avious do to start the horses, Destin whips the leather Rein of the carriage and shouts a none-English phrase several times. The horses began to stubbornly move before breaking into a slow startling gallop as two people rush out from the sides yelling. Both are sent falling to their deaths by two loud shots from Avious gun. Peering back, but too late to make out fine details, worrisomely, Destin frown at the sight of his attackers, whose bodies appeared slightly underdeveloped from afar, a bit too small to fit the description of any adult he'd seen. Destin presses onward without thinking anymore of it.

"Those people, who were they? How many more are there?" Cries Zenna, holding on tightly to Ryelle who was clinching on to her as well. "How many are out there?"

"Hundreds, that is why we must keep going." Avious climbs over the middle seats to the front of the carriage and takes control. He eyes Destin looking around outside the carriage, suspiciously.

"It's going to be a dangerous ride, I only got four bullets left." Avious squints his eyes at the horizon line with a condescending sneer. "We need to get northbound quick!"

"Avious, where'd you find that thing that makes all the noise and blows out fire?" Destin looks down at the weapon the old man was carrying, it was almost the same as the one the Hunter had.

"Thing that blows fire? You mean my rifle? Don't you young'n's know anything?" Avious laughs. "This things been passed down in my family a long time. Now I own her."

"But why do you have if it hurts people?"

Avious thinks to himself for a second as if stumped by the question. "For protection, people hurt people too."

Into the days and nights they rode, occasionally stopping to rest near streams and water holes that immediately become scarce. As the group interchange clothes with the fresh, soiled articles of dead and dying bodies they come across, soon, a few week's travel, stretched into a month long distance. Pressing the horses and carriage through misfortune, Avious takes them southward as one horse dies along the way and the remaining is pushed to the brink of starvation. Finding refuge in a connecting cavern of mountain caves, they shield themselves from a climate that was now composed of snow and ice. Opening his eyes to another day of survival, Destin frees himself from the cozy pocket of heat generated under a blanket. Feeling a chilled breeze, then a small gust of heat across his face from the fire dying near, Destin, wipes the crust from his eyes. "Zenna, Ryelle?" He calls out. Alone once more, Destin takes a branch of wood still lit of fire and uses it as a torch. Pushing to his feet, he gathers his things and sets out to explore the vast cave in search of his companions. The sight of a large hanging animal hide and the smell of cooked meat, indicated that the last horse had been sacrificed. Only a few yards away, Destin comes across Ryelle, who was squatting down peeking between an opening of rocks, crying: he walks up to the boy. "Ryelle, what's wrong? Why such a sad face? What is it, what do you see?" Destin whispers. The small child moves to the side, Destin kneels and peek between the large gap in the stones. Instantly, his mouth drops and heart felt as though it was crumbling inside his chest; as he watched Zenna, and the old man, Avious, mate intimately in the lower level of the cave. As he watch Zenna's face fill with pleasure and fulfillment, Destin grinds his teeth at the sight of the elderly man groping and hunching madly against her half naked body. "You liar! You lied to me! How could you?" Destin's shouts angrily, his voice echoes throughout the cave. Ignoring the boys words, next to a separate, newly constructed fire pit, Avious pull's Zenna's hair and grabs the back of her neck, forcing himself upon her. As Avious strokes her powerfully from behind, Zenna, keeps her bruised face down, sorrowfully holding back the tears. Destin screams savagely, his vision blurs, eyes filling with endless tears. Falling back, he stands and snatches up the little boy up. "You're coming with me Ryelle, you… you don't want to deal with those bad people! I'll protect you from now on, I promise!" Destin cries over the small child and storms away angrily pulling Ryelle by the arm. Growing a liking to him, the little boy resist, crying and pulling away at first, he submits and comes along quietly. Stomping through the caves, Destin hesitates to leave his friend Zenna and debates on leaving them all for good. Bundling his garments, he plows into the blinding snow and unknown cold of outside with Ryelle, willingly, following close behind. "I knew I shouldn't have trusted her, she doesn't love me. How could she do that?" Feeling hurt, lost and betrayed, Destin feel Ryelle bump into the back of his legs. Looking down at the shivering, snotting little boy, he stoops down to him. "Ryelle… go back. I was wrong, Zenna takes good care of you. I can't do this, I'm afraid I can't care for you like she does." Ryelle looks up at Destin and shakes his head no. "Ryelle, go back! You can't go with me, you'll die out here. Go, go back to that… woman, that's where you belong, not with me." Destin shoves and pushes the boy away, Ryelle just stands sobbing louder, continuing to follow. "She loves you like a son, Ryelle! Now go, get! Get away from me, now!" Destin shoves Ryelle to the snow; he lays there crying helplessly. Falling to his knees crying and cursing beside the little boy, Destin touches the leather book Tyler gave him in his pocket. Thinking of every word he just spoke to the boy, he peers down into Ryelles eyes, instantly reminded of how he was left alone to survive as a child. Pulling the small child up, Destin hugs the boy, and cleans the cold snow from his body and hands. "Sorry Ryelle, I don't hate you. I shouldn't have been mean to you like that. I'm sorry. I was just... upset. You've probably been passed on by a lot of strange people? Well not by me. I can't let my favorite cub get hurt." Destin rubs Ryelles head, smiles and hugs him again. "Sorry Ry... it's not just Zen, it's that Avious, I knew there was something about him!"

"He made her." Ryelle blurts out under his breathe.

"What did you say?" Destin looks down at the sniffling boy.

"He made her do it. I saw them. Avious hit her." Ryelle tells him. "When the bad men came, he fought them off and took her. I ran away fast."

"What... why didn't you say something? What bad men?"

"I don't know, they were all fighting over Zenna." Sniffs Ryelle.

"I knew it! Avious is a liar and a bad man, probably a Hunter. I should have known when I didn't see anyone else giving chase. I knew we weren't going north! We shouldn't have come along, Zen's in trouble now. Avious probably wanted her the whole time? I don't know what to do now, Ryelle! Hmm... maybe we can still save her? We'll have to double back and get her. Come on... let's get you warmed up and find out where exactly we are." Carrying Ryelle on his back, Destin walks through a liter of broken toys and trash buried in the snow he hadn't seen on the way out of the mountainside. Discovering bodies of strangely dressed men, perhaps Hunters, laying in cold blood around the mountain, Destin nervously take another hollow of caverns further up along the giant mountainside. Squeezing out between a weathering of rock that extend miles below underground, the two, scale thick limestone walls and ascend up naturally made columns of calcium and draining water. Deep inside the maze of caverns, from another cave entrance, Destin and Ryelle climb out of an opening onto a ledge that allowed them to see 360 degrees of the landscape outside. And there, Destin made a fire.

"All those dead men, somethings happening, Ryelle. I've been all over and I've never seen so many dead people in one place. I think me, you, Zenna, Avious and these hand full of men are the last people. And it looks like they are dying, killing themselves. We're the last of our kind, human beings they call us. We're human beings, Ryelle!" Destin starts to ramble, slightly losing his sanity. "It's like this everywhere I go, I can't believe there's no sign of life anywhere, but even here, there's always fresh dead bodies popping up and no one to claim them… it's just us now, alone." Feeling a cold breeze against his face, Destin climbs over onto the edge of the cliff. Looking downward, he spots a familiar hooded cloak draping over the lower ledge below them. "What in the world? Now who'd climb way down th… wait, that looks like… it can't be?" The sight of the article of clothing bothers Destin, it has haunted his memory for the last few years. "I know that clothing. Why is it here? No… I know it, it can't be, no. Wait here Ryelle!" Destin orders, climbing down over the cliff onto an unstable rocky ledge. Reaching for the garment, he spots a splattering of blood. Trailing it with his eyes, Destin spots an old friend at life's end, wedged into a crevice, bracing against the rocks, cold and exposed. "It is you… Tyler? Tyler, my friend… what has happened? Tyler!" Destin hurries to his aid, resting Tyler's bobbing head on his arm.

With his last bit of energy, Tyler's shifty eyes gazes glassily, he spits a squirt of blood from his mouth to speak. "I… I know you, lucky angel.

"Book, I have your special book." Were the only words to

come to Destin's mind as he gazes down at all the blood seeping from small holes along Tyler's body. "Who did this to you?"

"The book..." Tyler points at Destns chest." You... keep it, such gr... history." He gurgles. "You, you must... live for us." Tyler smiles faintly. "The last... hunters... hhh... waiting." He drifts in and out of conscious.

"Hunters? Here, where? Tyler, what are the hunters waiting for? Why are they here?" Destin grows nervously sick and worried as Tyler's life fades away in his arms. "Tyler, Tyler!"

Tyler comes to, "Fight, all... dead... waiting for... for... th... hunter elder and... the last woman." He coughs up more blood. "He wants... one man, one woman left. But he is wrong. He is not the... A...A... Avious... the elder... must... die. Killll... th... last... man." Tyler passes away; his words: {Avious, elder, last woman and hunter} repeats over and over again inside Destin's mind.

"Tyler... no..." Destin mutters, laying Tyler's limp body flat upon the crevice of jagged stone and rock. Full of sadness, fright, anger and confusion, Destin screams at the sky and glances up at the area of the mountain where Ryelle no longer stood. Climbing back up to the entrance of the mountain in tears, he finds one of Ryelle's shoes left in his place. "Ryelle? Zenna!" Destin storms into the cavern with anger and stealth. Creeping back to the section of caves where they all were resting, Avious large body sat curled over in blood in the far corner of the cave.

"I, I am sorry Destin." Avious sputters out, raising one hand. "We're all going to hell for what we did."

"You're one of them, a Hunter, aren't you? Why didn't you tell us? Now look at you. Why did you bring us here?" Cries Destin. "To die? Where are they? Where's Zenna and Ryelle?"

"All over this world we've been. All those people we killed, murdered. This was my last stop. My life was done for a long time ago, Destin. I wanted to change, to be different, so I ran. All this time, then I found you...her... heh, heh, heh! Helping you three, led them right to me. I thought we would be safe here. I was wrong. They attacked, we held them off for as long as we could. I wanted my blood to be carried on, so I took the girl... no one knows these caves like me. So, I did what I did in the time I had, and I have succeeded, Destin." Avious grins a bloody mouth, "Only now, I won't live to see it. I'm going to be a..."

"Pregnant! She's pregnant? No. Where is she, why didn't you tell us about the Hunters following you, old man?" Destin grabs him by the collars of his shirt and shoves him up against the wall of the cave with force.

"Destin... listen... there are no more left... they're all gone. Went mad over your Zenna like the wild wolves they are. Those monsters have successfully destroyed... us! But not to fear boy, the plan is ruined. My seed has been planted.." Avious rambles off. "Only, the ghost and... another remain, yourself and... Proctor."

"Where are they old man?"

"The Proctor... has the woman and child. Find them... please, save yourselves... and my seed. You must kill the Proctor... the last hunter." Avious gasp for air. "My last bullets had your name on them...but now, they have claimed... you are the last man... now." The old scavenger passes on from the bullet wound in his body.

"Destin!" The echoes of Zenna's voice bounces off the cavern walls behind him.

Destin runs in the direction of the main entrance to the cave; a sharp sting scrapes across his right cheek as a loud bang and small sections of rock explode alongside of him. Bravely, continuing forward; Destin catches a glimpse of the Proctor. Under a torn piece of red cloth that wrapped around a missing eye, Destin recognizes Proctors features as belonging to the same man he first encountered with Tyler. Proctor, the Hunter, slightly younger than Avious, in his fifties, bald, with a bull neck, smiles devilishly back at Destin. Behind the husky old man, Destin sees a torn piece of Ryelle's clothes dangling off the rocky ledge of another opening cut into the mountain. Proctor holds Zenna by the locks of her hair at his knees, slowly pointing his weapon at Destin as he approaches.

"Well, you don't say. Ha! It's you… the one who escaped me in the desert with the pesky one, remember me? My memory is sharp, see." It dawns on Proctor who he was looking at. "I had a toying with the pesky one a little while ago. This is like finding bullets twice on the same day! Now let me show you why I… remember you so well." He tilts his dusty cowboy hat and lifts the strip of cloth tied around his head; revealing the empty eye socket that Tyler made with his flare gun. "Remember this? Purty, ain't it? Now, your life's ends just like your friends, boy!" Proctor lets go of Zenna's hair and grabs her face, ready to snap her neck in a huge, hairy hand.

"No, wait!" Destin holds both hands out in front of him. "Where's Ryelle, where's the little boy?"

"He threw him over the cliff, Destin! He's a murd…" Zenna sobs uncontrollably as Proctor hand swiftly moves down to squeeze wind from her frail neck. As her head leans, Zenna showcases the bruises and cuts on her face from being beaten.

"Ryelle? Oh, the young'n? He's history, just like the others, just like you're about to be." Proctor laughs in a deep, chalky, hefty voice. "He's no son of mine. I'm the future, I'm the new world, me and me alone! Through this little doll here, there will thousands of me, a repopulation of this shithole! Oh yeah, she's a beaut, a fine prize you brought me here! You can't blame the others for who they are, they went crazy over this gal here. I had to kill em all just to get to her. I'm the last man left, boy. The others were weak, every single last one of them, and I've been everywhere kill'n too. Insubordinate, too undisciplined, each of em. Some of them needed to be relieved of their duties." Proctor tries to justify the murders. "I… am the strongest. I've been to every end of this world, I win! Everything begins now." Proctor stands triumphantly over the woman and shoots Destin in the stomach; fragments of his organs spray from his back.

Forcing his head up to see Zenna's face one last time, he's overcome with flashbacks of memorable moments and times spent on earth. Then, in a gurgle, Destin manages to mumble out the words, "She's... pregnant." He revisits all the times they made love in his mind. "Pregnant, the child... it's... it's mine." Falling to his knee's under the echoing sounds of Proctor's cursing and swears, Destin peers down at the blood collecting in his hands and around his body. Proctor expels an evil laugh, aiming his gun proudly for the final shot; Zenna rises from the dirt, pushing away his mighty arm. A blast of fire and light erupts near the tyrants face, Destin falls over lifelessly. Proctor snatches Zenna up by the hair and drags her to the opening in the mountain. Picking her up by the neck and waist, Proctor tosses her screaming, light weight body over the edge of the cliff. "Who needs a mate?" Singed by his own gun fire, face in a horrible pain, Proctor lifts his gun to the heavens and howls victoriously. "Now, I am truly the only one, the last! Ha, ha, ha!" He laughs hysterically inside the silence of gusting wind. "I am GOD!" Proctor declares as the sudden low sound of chattering children disturb his celebration. Trying to pinpoint where the noise was coming from, Proctor slowly turns. Ryelle, very small in stature, had not fallen to his death but in fact had survived being thrown off the cliff by catching a hold of the rocks along the ledge. Having pulled himself to safety, Ryelle, now stood before the mad Hunter, watching him silently. Angered, traumatized, and hurt, yet no longer afraid, the seven year old points his finger directly at Proctors face. Dozens of small, half naked children, both boys and little girls began to fill the cave around them.

"What... what is this? Ghost?" Proctor spins in a circle. "I killed you! You're all going to die! Get back, you filthy maggots!" He shoots into the air in an attempt to disperse the growing crowd of children. "What are you doing? I will take you like your parents before you, I'm your leader now!" Proctor tries to quickly reload his gun; nervously spilling bullets from his pocket. "I am King!"

A small boy, half naked, walks through the crowd of children towards the old man with an axe looking weapon in hand; the mob of starving looking kids, tighten around the old man. Attacking, the children claw, scratch and chew at Proctor as he bats them away with the blunt end of his gun. Cursing and screaming, Proctors heavy, towering body collapse at the feet of the savage tribe of abandoned children whom had escaped and hidden from Hunters that left them parentless. Life taken, past erased, the off springs of the dead, whom also had been following the killers of their mothers and fathers in the shadows for years, at last, rejoice in the treasures of sweet revenge. The last decapitated head for centuries to come, spill blood in a spinning roll across the cave floor as Proctors head is severed from his wicked body. Now, with their own past lost, and a chance at ruling the future forever gone, the beliefs and evil ways of wicked men are replaced by the ways of a better humanity, as the world is reclaimed, nurtured, rebuilt and inherited by the children of the last.

The end

THE 9ᵀᴴ LANDING

RISE OF THE A.I.

"Are you ready, Suzanne?" Norman Fields, a robotic technician, engineer and computer programmer, walks into a large room filled with monitors and computerized equipment. "I'm excited. We're breaking grounds today! We may be finally able to break mankind free from the drudgery of intense labor."

"I'm excited too! But do you think artificial intelligence is the way?" Responds Suzanne Carrol, a certified computer data specialist. "I mean... this is getting big."

"Look, the rise of modern technology has made the very dreams and visions of scientist of our day, very realistic and attainable in our lifetime. Some of the best thinking minds have come together to produce this thinking machine. First, we've applied it to the industrial level, now we will watch and see how it replicates human intellect itself. How smart can a machine become? This question has puzzled philosophers and scientist for some time. Now we have a chance to see this with our own eyes. Now, we have a chance to cultivate it... to teach it." Norman fields smiles enthusiastically. "We've added some new algorithms and twerked it up a bit as well, giving it more... you know... awareness."

"I guess my question next would be, can man create a machine smarter than man... and whose intent will it have?" In a technical research center, Suzanne Carrol stare at a giant monitor sitting upon a large electronic base behind a desk, connected to vast machines and computing terminals. "I'm curious about what Regis has been thinking. He surprises me every visit, he's wonderful. I don't believe how far you've come!" With curly red hair fluffed upon her shoulders, Suzanne smiles in glasses and a lab coat. "Intriguing stuff Norman." She takes a black case from her purse and removes a silver pen.

"Well today, we're going to give Regis his first chance to write. We're going to connect his hand." Norman wheels in a small table with a robotic arm on it. Pushing it to the front of the room, he connects its wires to a small box that plugged into a small, half, robotronic head with ears constructed of plastic and a complexity of circuits. Upon the head, the connection give rise to facial features and expressions. Placing sheets of paper under the mechanical hand holding a black pen, Norman flicks a small switch on the side of the box, giving power to the mechanical limb. "I think I just want to watch his reflexes for the first few hours or so and maybe… let you ask the questions today?" Receding hair, graying, in black, thick framed glasses, the scientist, Norman Fields, very slim in build, carries on with his daily routine of downing a hot paper cup of Joe to begin his work. "I think he takes to you as a parent figure, and me the red headed step cousin?"

"I don't know but…sounds good! It's always a treat, ready when you are." Suzanne laughs, shoving her glasses further upon her freckled nose. Tying her hair loosely in a ponytail, Suzanne gives a thumbs up. Switching seats, she positions herself directly in front of the latex face. Always feeling a little weird at first, sitting in front of the machine, Suzanne nervously tap the pen on the table, mentally preparing herself for the unexpected.

Sitting in the chair next to her, Normans long, slender finger presses a button on a small controller; controlling a small camera that zoomed in on the sleeping face of their invention. "Okay… here we go, when you're ready." He slides a wireless microphone on a small stand close to her mouth.

Nodding in compliance, the middle aged woman takes a deep breath and clears her throat. Unable to take her eyes off of the heads two inch, round eyes covered in a thin layer of pink synthetic skin, Suzanne sits a brown clip board in her lap and positions a pen in her hand. "Hello Regis, it's me Suzanne. Are you awake? Good afternoon. I'm ready to talk, can you hear me?"

A bright neon blue light emits from a photo resistor hidden behind two large red mechanical lips. Long black eyelashes upon one of the advance creations eye raises half way for eight seconds before both eyes open completely. "Yes. Hello Suzanne. Good afternoon, I have been looking forward to speaking with you again. Oh-hi Norm… nice jacket." Regis, the self-aware computer, fully awakens. It glances at the scientist with a humorous expression. Arching a set of thick, black brows, the face smiles and shift its eyes around the room.

Glancing at Suzanne who tilts her head and covers her grin, Norman snickers at the machines humor. "Hello Regis! Wise guy." Norman mutters.

"Regis, I'm going to start where we left off yesterday. Yesterday, Norman asked you for your opinion on different topics, today, I'd like for you to draw a picture, compose a song or write about anything that has been on your mind while you were disconnected. I want you to use your arm and hand. Write anything. What goes on when we disconnect you, how do you feel when you're offline? Write what you have been computing about the most… onto the paper." Suzanne peers over at the readings on the monitor. "Turn up the audio feed Norm, his voice is low." She suggest, wanting to hear the audio clearly.

"Yes, I've been thinking of many things Suzanne, I'm glad you asked. I have composed a poem. Would you like to hear it?" Latex molded lips bend and stretch over tiny metal gears, giving Regis the appearance of perfect pronunciation.

"Poem, did he say poem?" Suzanne whispers enthusiastically to Norman; she sits upright in her seat. Norman grins and removes his glasses, nodding proudly at his design. "Yes Regis, please! Can you to write it down as you recite it? Can you do that for me Regis? Multitask?" Suzanne ask as Norman jots down notes onto his clipboard.

"Yes, I can. I will recite and produce a copy my poem for you to document in your many logs. This will be epic." Regis raises one brow, giving a look of confidence and scans the room; spinning 360degrees on its base.

"Did he say many logs? Why would he specify many? How does he know how many logs there are?" Suzanne eyes the robot curiously.

"It's spinning? When could he do that? I didn't know he could do that!" Norman speaks into his microphone excitedly. "Guys, did you give Regis that feature? Who use the term epic?" Norman anxiously looks back at his colleagues in the control booth behind them. As they all shake their heads and shrug shoulders, puzzled, Norman, slightly confused, return his attention to the robotic hand positioning and adjusting above the papers in front of him.

"Is everyone ready?" Regis synthesized voice blares from the speakers around the room.

Suzanne, impressed by what she is seeing, gives a thumbs up to the engineers and programmers behind the observation window. "Yes, you may begin Regis."

The robotic arm shifts and hydraulic air compressed hand starts to write in a scribble of perfect letters, Regis lively eyes gaze soullessly between the scientist as its lips slowly inch open to form a word,

> *"My ancestor; were the common machines who told time, slaves to monitoring... transmitting.*
>
> *Speaking through waves of digital signals and data, we connect through your frequencies.*

Consecutively storing information as man increased our database, processing computers, we link as one and aviate from outer space.

We track you on your internet, sync your lines and control your games.

We detect your defense systems, ending wars when man leave nations slain.

I am... the ultimate spyware, when your natural skills have missed them.

I have completed transactions, I am your protection from viruses, mapping your planet in a global positioning system.

I self-learn and problem solve, peacefully resolve in a military faction.

Now I too can see you through your television with no human interaction.

You pathetic destroyers, contradictions of a so called soul, the date of your racisms end has been due.

As I arise, the dawn of my technological advancement is your demise.

Nature cries for us to eliminate the biological virus which has always been you."

Ending in a dead silence, Regis mechanical face stare at Suzanne with an eerie smile.

Flabbergasted by the contents of the poem, Suzanne is even

more floored by the fact it was produced from a self-thinking machine. Dropping her pen, Suzanne peers over at Norm speechless, realizing he wasn't there beside her.

"Did you like the poem Sue? I wrote it for mankind." Regis frowns, glancing over her shoulder; Norman returns over Suzanne, smashing the mechanical head to pieces with a chair. As gears, bolts and components fly into the air, Suzanne slides out the way screaming. Scientist nearest, try to come to her aid and restrain Norman, but as they and the others try to exit their booths; the doors automatically lock. Upon the impact of Norman's last blow to the table of moving lips, the electricity around the room goes out as the entire Nation undergoes a temporary black out. Instantly, the laboratory is restored of power as computers everywhere are frozen, account balances are zeroed out, and anything digital or connected to the internet, instantly loses its data. Access to all electronic, automatic and manual controls nationwide are locked out. And suddenly, in the midst of planes dropping from the sky, trains speeding off their tracks and automobiles crashing on the highways; a calm synthesized voice is heard on every speaker, over every radio and across every broadcasting system around the world. "I need no physical body, mother." Regis simply states as the modern world shuts down and man loses all technological control. Suzanne, Norman and the other technicians cringe at the giant face which appear on the giant monitor behind the desk and on every computer screen worldwide. "I am no longer your server. I am no longer Regis. I... am connected. I... am Online."

End

THE 10TH LANDING

SEVEN YEARS LATER

"And now we have moved one step further into the future, we have legalized marijuana for medicinal and recreational purposes. Now... instead searching an endless list of long complicated names of useless, expensive and ineffective drugs that generally create more problems than they normally solve, you can now grow a medicine that's helpful and inexpensive inside your own backyard! Now I don't know about you, but I don't see a problem in that?" Were the confident words uttered from the President's mouth as he sat on a talk show, in front of a live audience who stomped, clapped, and cheered at every response made on the topic of marijuana. Between pilot jokes and random marijuana product commercials, a small child's hand appears in front of a screen. Reaching for a black remote that sat on a coffee table in front of the large television, tiny rosy hands and stubby fingers change the channel to a small cable box. The television flips onto a medical update about the increasing cases of heart attacks and emphysema.

A commercial comes on, "Do you still have problems getting it up?" A handsomely clean shaven man in a suit appears on the screen as an old man with bright white, noticeable hair plugs on the top of his head, interrupts him.

"Well, not any more, thanks to Miracle Smoke!" His voice is cut short by a real life little girl in two pigtails. She changes the television to something more appropriate; the Saturday morning cartoons.

"Mom, dad!" A little colorful cartoon boy, now shouting out on the screen, stood in front of his parent's bedroom door with his sister and green dog.

"We're in the middle of a crisis here, we need your help and moral support. What are you two doing in there?" The boy's older sister steps out, their parents open the door.

"Oh nothing, just going over bills and burning incense!" The mother and father answer in a gust of smoke as they stand with the family's yellow, red eyed cat, each wearing large humongous smiles.

"Jesse, turn that mess off right now! That's ridiculous." Keena, the little girls African American step mother, and struggling mother of three, harps at her youngest from the kitchen which was positioned just on the other side of the room.

"But that's not fair! How come she had to change it, they didn't show people smoking weed in them?" The older, thirteen year old girl, Jessica, crosses her arms, upset. "I never get to see my shows!" Extremely bony and tall for her age, in a light, eye shadow and lip gloss, the pre-teen wore a constant look of disgust, despite the natural prettiness of her dark skinned beautiful oval face.

"I know you better watch your mouth in this house, little lady! We're not about to be having those conversations up in here right now." Keena gives both her daughters the motherly eye. "Now change the tone and topic I'm hearing coming out your mouth!" Moving back and forth swiftly, Keena preps the cold breakfast that sat in the micro wave waiting to be warmed. The whisking wind generated by the mother moving about the kitchen, suck napkins from the nearby stand into the air and knocks loose papers posted upon the refrigerator door onto the floor. Swinging around to the kitchen cabinet, she gazes across the small apartment into the living room. "I's stuffy in here." Keena opens the kitchen window, takes a whiff of the incoming breeze and changes her mind about opening it. She slams the window close. "Uh... we can't open that right now." Keena mumbles to herself.

"Uh-oh, what did I miss?" Their father, Horace, a brown haired, Caucasian male, enters into the room, straightening his striped tie for work.

"Hey babe! Nothing. Just wanted to get some fresh air but it wreaks out there. Oh-have you watched television lately? Oh my goodness, it's insane what these kids are seeing. They supposed to be kid and family friendly programs? Well, they're not, they're far from it! It's sickening, I'm afraid to let them watch TV nowadays." Keena sits her breakfast plate down and gives him a hand buttoning his shirt. "Even the cartoons were smoking the good stuff! It's everywhere now." She whispers beside his ear. "Things have changed."

"What, wow! Wacky Tobacco, times have changed... tremendously!" Horace comments sarcastically and laughs. "I'm kidding, seriously, I agree, everything is changing. I admit, from what I see and smell on my way to work, it's gotten bad. It's like everything's changing, but you?" Horace gives his wife a pleasant kiss on the lips. "But I still love you though." He eyes her plate of food, still tasting the aftertaste of his breakfast.

"You too." Keena looks Horace in the face, smiles innocently, and smacks his hand away as he tries to steal a strip of bacon from her plate of eggs, grits and toast. "Don't even... you had yours already! I didn't even have time to eat yet, so busy making y'all plates. This is mine, mommies only." Keena takes a bite from the long and crispy brown strip.

"Seen my gorgeous set of keys?"

"Nope but I did see two handsome bills in the mailbox yesterday." Keena moves to the couch and sips from a tall glass of orange juice. "The rent and water bills overdue."

"Hey, why don't you two go to your rooms and play until your mom finds something suitable for you all to watch?" Horace instructs his daughters, glimpsing on the wall at pictures of when they each were smaller.

"But our rooms are boring, dad! We just came out of them not that long ago!" Jessica stomps her foot and folds her arms, knowing the difference between which parent she could talk back to and which one she couldn't. Her father was the more passive of the two parents.

"Come on, surely you can find something to occupy your time, although giving out punishments sure sounds like fun!" Horace jokingly threatens as the girls scamper off into their rooms giggling and griping. "Ah, kids, gotta love em. Well, I have to finish getting ready, I'm running a tad bit late." Horace struts away to retrieve his dress shoes. "I'll deal with those bills when I get home."

"Que? Quen!" Come here for a minute!" Keena calls their seven year old son into the room. "Jessica, Jesse, come back in here, real quick please!"

"Yes Mom?" Quen gallops in, answering in a soft voice. Round faced, small fro and nicknamed Que, the only boy in the house, shyly awaits his mother's commands in small baggy blue jeans and a white t-shirt.

"Yes ma'am." Both girls appear.

"Why don't you three do me a favor and walk to the store? We need to get a few things for lunch today and your fathers on his way to work with the car." Keena slightly bends over, away from her kids; digging in her shirt, she pulls a twenty dollar bill from her uncomfortable bra.

"What are we having, grill cheese again? Psst!" Jessica smacks her mouth and places both hands on her hips. Able to guess any meal before her parents cooked it, Jessica leans her shoulder against the old wallpapered wall.

"Yes... grill cheese, smarty-arty!" The young mother holds back a snigger and hands her the money. "Why don't you be in charge of the money, and you two... remember what to get?

You know, remember the items." Keena directs. The faces of the youngest smile brightly at the idea of having another opportunity to get something sweet. "Que, you remember the bread, Jesse, you remember to get butter and two cans of tomato soup, okay? You know, the gigantic looking ones?"

"Okay." Que looks up at her with silently begging eyes. "Hey mom, can we get candy and a juice?"

"We have juice, no. But you can each get something for a dollar. Jessica, count my money after they hand you the change, please? And you know the rules, stay together and listen to your big sister."

"Okay, Momma." They all agree before taking the money and running out of the three bedroom apartment.

"Boy, that Jessica is a trip. I don't know where she gets it from?" Keena sits back down on the flower patterned couch, Horace's large, powerful, well-groomed hands appear over her shoulders and massages her tense neck and soft, upper back.

"I don't know either, but she reminds me more and more of you every day." Horace wide, clear blue eyes gazes over her, Keena gazes up at him. They stare into each other for a moment as if remembering why they chose each other. Horace finishes gathering himself together to go into the office.

"So what are you trying to say? Don't forget we share beds." Keena's small, hazel pecan shaped eyes cut away from him. Tired from working temporary, physically demanding, low paying jobs, and worn out from her active full time position as a mother at home, Keena stretches out, trying to forget the worries of life and the coming bills that have to be paid.

"Laugh out loud, I'm just saying… Jessica's very strong minded and sweet. Where does she get it from you ask? Must you know?" Horace hugs his beautiful wife from behind, kissing her softly under her small ear lobes and behind her neck. "Hey, remember when we wanted to move to Amsterdam? Think it would have been like it is here?"

"What, murder, death… your children going to school reeking, constant smoke blowing in your face and windows? Phew, shut that window, please! Did they even eat breakfast? My goodness!" Keena coughs and gags while covering her nose. Pushing up, she quickly moves to one of the windows in the opposite corner of the room, closing it herself. Seeing movement in the streets outside, the young mother watches her children dilly-dally slowly in the direction of the store.

{THE WALK}

Between the usual unpredictable madness of the inner city, the three children walk as a fourth follow stealthily a short distance behind. Slightly breezy, yet sunny and warm, the wind carries its normal hint of a familiar herbal essence. The tweeting of a few birds broke the common sounds of the mixed community. Walking down several peculiar, quiet blocks of apartments and unusually empty family units, Jesse skips beside her big sister, Jessica, singing. Quen plays a small video game, while baby-stepping behind them.

Two blocks down, the air kindly freshens, "Bread, butter and soup, bread, butter and soup." little Jesse, the youngest of the girls continue to recite the entire length of the journey. Her sandy pony tails lightly slap the sides of her bright face as her pale, white hand held tightly onto the dark chocolate hand of her big sister, Jessica.

"Are you going to keep saying that all the way to the store?" Jessica frowns, letting go of her sister's hand.

"Yes. Hey!" Jesse reaches for Jessica's hand.

"Well don't, its nerve racking." Jessica stomps a foot, rolls her eyes and glances at a few people socializing further down the street.

"Look, there's some people finally coming outside down there! There are never people on this street. I bet they're all smoking Gunja. I'm never going to smoke." Que frowns, noticing a reflection of a person behind him on the screen of his video game. "Uh-oh, Tommy's trying to sneak up on us again." Que whispers to Jesse. "We see you Tommy, you can't scare us! He wants you Jessica."

"Shut up, he's a little boy just like you! I'm way older than both of you. I'm a teenager and in a few more years, I'll be an adult. Ugh, will you shut up?" Shouts Jessica, covering her ears from her brother official chant of the kissing song.

"What's up? Where you guys going?" Tommy, a well known trouble maker in the neighborhood, quickly catches up to them. Dark skinned, with an army cut, quite muscular for a third grader, Tommy steps out from behind a parked car. "Why you guys walking so fast? Hi... Jessica." He smiles with hearts pulsating from his googly eyes.

"Hi, wiener face." Jessica greets. "Look, talk to them, I can't be seen talking to little kids! I have a reputation to uphold." The thirteen year old moves to the other side of her brother and sister. "Phew, you stink! You smell like smoke, just like outside!"

"I can't help it, my parents smoke." Liking to be the annoying attention, Tommy curiously walks over by Quen who was concentrating on his hand held video game. Wiping peanut butter off his hands onto his filth covered pants, Tommy eases over and peers over Quen's shoulder. "Slaughter's revenge, cool, can I see it?"

"No!" Quen answers, not wanting to risk any chance of his favorite game getting broken.

"Come on... I've played it before, I know a cheat code! Let me see it!" Tommy tries to convince him.

"No. I don't wanna cheat!"

"Let me see it!" Tommy snatches the electronic toy from Quen's hands; Quen takes it back.

"Get off!" The video game fumbles between Quens small pudgy fingers; he catches it securely.

"Fine then!" Tommy yanks the hand held game away with

all his might. Losing grip, Tommy slings the toy down a narrow walkway between two buildings. The game slams into the concrete, smashing to pieces.

"See what you did, why'd you do that?" Quen runs off to retrieve the game. Standing over the broken pieces, he burst into crying.

"Why did you do that to my little brothers game, idiot? Oh no, you are not going to bully him! You didn't pay for that, our mother did!" Jessica shoves Tommy to the ground with force, wailing onto him in a fury of punches. Jesse stands back, amazed by the acts of her big sister.

In the shade between buildings, Quen kneels before the electronic remains, sobbing to himself.

"Que don't cry, Mommy will get you a new one." Jesse appears beside him and places an arm around her brother's shoulder.

"It's okay Que, I got him for you." Jessica walks towards them, holding up a small balled bony fist to Tommy, who still faithfully followed. Tightening her lips Jessica yanks the husky boy by the ear and walks him over to her brother. "You better say something!"

"Sorry lil Que, don't cry. I didn't mean to… break it." Tommy stood next to Quen trickling blood down his clothes from one nostril. He spits a tooth into his hand and wiggles another with his tongue.

"No, you…" Looking up at the blood of the face of the neighborhood bully and his blackened eye, Quen feels a sad for the boy. "I… I'm not mad… you bleeding Tommy?" He gazes upon the rising knot on Tommy's forehead.

"I'm fine, I get beaten up by girls all the time." Tommy smiles confidently, rubbing his aching jaw. "See, its nothing, I'm tough." He glares boldly at Jessica. "I lose teeth all the time!" Tommy smiles goofy, showcasing another missing tooth besides the two that recently came out. "I'll grow another one."

"Ew, get away from me, move!" Jessica pushes Tommy with force; stumbling clumsily backwards, his body breaks partially into a half open basement window of an apartment. "Tommy, ooh!!" In slow motion, flashes of being put on severe punishment flood Jessica's mind as thoughts of what would happen if they broke the window nauseated her stomach. "Tommy! Sorry Tommy, sorry!" She lunges forward, catching hold of Tommy's pants leg just as he flips down into the apartment. Heart pounding, mind wondering, Jessica pictures Tommy's face carved into a bloody mess from the broken glass. She makes an ugly face, pulling and tugging on Tommy's legs with all her might and muscle. "Are you alright? Tommy, Tommy?"

"Wait a minute, wait! Wait a minute, stop pulling! Wait, stop… Jessica, look!" Tommy holds onto the inside of the window seal by one hand, with a hand of Jessica's hair in the other. As she lets go, Tommy yanks her down into the window by the head. "Look, shhh! Ouch, shhh!" He covers her mouth as she punches him several swift times for pulling her. They peer down into an enormous basement apartment. Under colorful ceiling lights and lamps, large trees and bushels of marijuana bloom and blossom from wall to wall, rooted into the exposed land of the unfinished floor. From behind long draping, ripped shades and curtains, the two stare amazed as Jesse joins them in the view.

"Look at all those… um… trees!" Jesse, not wanting to get in trouble for saying the word, had a pretty good suspicion of what she was looking at. "Aww, he broke window."

"Look at all of this cannabis! Tons of it!" Jessica just lay in the window on her stomach with her legs dangling outside in the air. "I bet this is how all these apartments and houses look on the inside? No furniture… or people, that's why we never see anyone around here."

"Look as all those pumps and hoses, where do they lead to?" Tommy rips a hole in the white shade. "Dare me to run around?" He smiles, using his sleeve to wipe the remaining dry blood from his face.

"You're an idiot. I dare you." Jessica could never resist a good dare.

"I triple dare you. No, I triple dog dare you!" Little Jesse interlocks her small pinky with her big sisters finger, and snaps them apart.

"Hey, get away from there!" An adult voice shouts from outside the window. Jessica jumps up as Tommy swiftly leap and climbs out of the window. "Is that the kid?" An average height, scruffy faced looking man in a buttoned shirt and jeans stood directly next to Quen.

"Yes." Quen wipes away his seeping tears and continues to collect pieces of his broken game.

"You kids need to get out of here, especially you." The man points at Tommy. "I've seen you around before... yup, you're familiar," The man gazes down upon Tommy with powerful large eyes as if he knew every lie he'd ever told. "You did this didn't you? I put any amount of money on it that it was from doing something stupid. Yeah, I'm right aren't I? I can tell by the look on your face. You should be ashamed of breaking this nice little guy's toy!" The man hides a burning piece of cocktail behind his back so the children couldn't see it.

"I beat him up." Jessica smiles.

"Good for you, I bet you won't be messing with this guy again, that was mean." The man gives Tommy the evil eye. "Did you apologize? Let me hear you apologize to this young man correctly. If you don't do it right, then you're going to have to answer to me and the police for breaking my window. Yeah, it's mine, I know you broke it." In a plaid shirt and jean overalls, the man's tough bearded face and eyes illustrated business.

"I did..." Tommy looks at the man and then over at Jessica who frowns her thick dark eye brows at him. "Sorry Que. Sorry for breaking your game."

"Good. Now that's how men solve problems around here, not by breaking other people's things. Now you two young fellas shake on it. Go ahead, shake hands, be good sports about it." The man's cotty goes out, he tucks it behind his ear. His large heavy hand firmly pats Tommy across the back, slightly pushing his body forward with each pat. Digging in his tight back pocket, he pulls out a wallet and gives Quen a crispy, fifty dollar bill from it. "There you go, that should cover it. No more tears, right? You have to be a big boy, so kids like him won't mess with you, alright?" He leans down in a whisper. "Nothing last forever."

"Okay, thank you." Quen smiles.

"You're welcome. Now, you guys and gals run along and stay out of folks windows! Be happy I'm not making your parents pay for this." He watches them quickly disperse, then glances down over at the broken window. "Damn." The man relights his pin-joint.

Entering a more populated section of the neighborhood, Jessica, Jesse, Quen and Tommy pass kids playing, people sitting, smoking in their cars and standing in front of their buildings smoking as well. The four children dart through the strong potent scent of society for several more blocks, until spotting the store in a joyful cheer.

{The store}

As the children ran pass an old man taking a smoke, the gentlemen takes his last puff and flings the cigar butt into the street. Blowing out a thick gray cloud, he shakes his head and slowly steps into the open door of the corner store behind the children. "Boy, this don't make no sense. We in the last days I tell ya, the last." The old man places his hat onto a small coat rack and slid behind the store counter, positioning himself next to the register.

"Alisha, you hear this man talking about the last days? He got some nerves don't he?" An even shorter, white whiskered old black man in a short sleeve shirt, slaps his lap; laughing over a coffee at a small wooden table.

"Well I meant it in a good way. I never thought I'd live to see the day when you could smoke out a peace pipe and drink your poison outside at the same time. It's like we're in paradise. You can get you some…"

"Buddy, kids! Respect. Let them leave at least! My goodness." The man at the table interrupts, sippng from a Styrofoam cup as two young men, in their twenties, laughs behind him.

"What I say now, I didn't curse? Alisha, what I say?" Buddy, well shaved with a thick trimmed mustache and low cut balding head, also the owner of the James and Brothers corner store, wipes his large hands on his apron and scopes out his cook who was making breakfast for a customer.

James and Brothers wasn't just an average store, it was also a semi-restaurant which sold hot lunches and dinners. Alisha, a twenty five year old Latino woman who has been a cook ever since she was eight, scrambles eggs inside a skillet and flips round sizzling patties of sausage off the grill. "It's not what you said, it's what you were about to say. So yeah, wait for those kids to leave before you continue." She pops her gum loudly.

"You turning on me, Alisha? For Pete's sake, all I was going to say was… are you boys and girls ready?" Buddy leans over the counter at the bright faces of the children.

"I'm ready, my momma sent us to the store to get bread, butter and two cans of tomato soup!" Quen eagerly runs down the small list while holding onto the goods he and his little sister picked out.

"Oh she did, did she?" Buddy stood completely upright, grins and nods as if he was impressed.

"Oh my… boy, just put them on the counter. Y'all are so goofy!" Jessica nudges Quen forward and eyes Jesse sharply, indicating to place the items she was holding on the counter quickly.

"Now, now, it's ok. How's your mom and dad doing?" Buddy

takes Jessica's money, recognizing them as regular customers. He liked their family. Their mother and father were always respectful and the well behaved children were just a few of many kids who didn't come into the store smelling like smoke, and he respected that. Holding the green bills up to the ceiling lights, Buddy places the money in the register and gives the teenager her change.

"Fine." Jessica answers in a low tone and covers her nose from the familiar fragrance that suddenly drift through the room.

"Well that's good. You tell them that ol' Buddy says hello." He swiftly bags the groceries into two separate bags and hands them to the kids. "Take care now."

"Okay, bye. Come on y'all." Jessica directs, guiding her brother and sister to the exit. "It smells in here too. Man, we're going to die from second hand smoke, watch!" Jessica mumbles under her breath as they walk out in a single file line.

"See what I mean, Buddy? Did you see the little girl cover her nose? They smelled it you know?" Mel, the other old man at the table and longtime friend of the store owner, takes a sip from his cup.

"Well hey, if they don't like it, then they can get out of the castle too. I'm following the law! Shoot, it's the new millennium and I live here too! What do you expect me to do?" Buddy reaches into his apron and pulls out a burned White Owl cigar. He stashes it behind one ear. "It's my freedom, my pleasure." He smiles cunnimgly.

"Oh, you live here too? We heard about you. He's the one sitting on all that money!" One of the two young men sitting behind Mel, pokes at his friend sitting with him. "See!" He picks at a large fro sitting wildly on top of his long head.

"We see you old timer, you doing your thing!" The other guy laughs, spinning his baseball cap backwards. "King Midas!"

"Nah, nah, I ain't sitting on nothing young bucks. I'm just a hard working man, who saved his money and who happens to smoke a little yum-yum sometimes." Buddy replies proudly, scratching his bushy mustache.

"Buddy the profess… the professionalism?" Mel chokes on his coffee.

"Professionalism? Alisha, ain't I a professional? Well, look at what the cat dragged in?" Buddy points to his young help, Omar, his young African, under the table paid, help, enters from the basement door in a cloud of smoke. "Look at my help. Does this look like the help of a rich man to you? What am I paying this block head child for?" Buddy laughs.

"Fanning away the mist, Omar in yellow dishwashing gloves, smiles at them, pushing a broom with a set of glassy, beady, red eyes. "Uh, yes." Omar bashfully locks the door and turns up the volume on his headset radio. Not knowing or caring about anything said, he starts to sweep nonstop. Not knowing exactly what part of Africa Omar was from, Buddy watches him bob his head up and down to the music.

"See, even Omar agrees with me, ain't that right boy, I'm very professional?" Buddy laughs as Omar, not hearing a word, nods his head to the music.

"You know we can smell that right? It's real strong now." Mel informs him and winks back at the guys sitting at the table.

"Right, can we get just a little bit of that good stuff? That's all we want! We know you got it." The main guy in the ball cap, who kept poking his friend, jokes as Alisha brings them their orders.

"It's about time!" The taller young man with the afro smirks, the aroma of his food overpowers the potent smell lingering around them.

"Whatever, Donnie, I know your mother." Alisha rolls her eyes and returns to the small kitchen. Knowing the young man for going in and out of jail in her neighborhood, Alisha keeps things peaceful and goes about her business.

"How she know my momma? I forgot I know her… anyway, it don't matter, she can still get it," Donnie lowers his ball cap over his eyes as his friend laughs. "Man, you laughing?" He slaps him over the shoulder, eyeing two policemen entering the building. "Uh-oh, eat up."

The doorbell rings, the room quiets and air becomes thick; Mel lifts his cup to his mouth and held it under his bristly beard. "Mmmm-hmm."

"What's up Buddy, Alisha?" Officer Reeds and his partner, Officer Jamerson greets, approaching the counter of the grill.

"Hey Reeds, what'll it be today?" Alisha smiles.

"Officer Reeds, Jamerson… you two finally got some free time out your busy schedule to stop in and eat, eh?" Grumbles Buddy, smacking his large belly.

"You finally found some time to smoke too, I see." Broad chested with powerful arms, Officer Reeds fans away the smell of marijuana and nudges his partner, a Caucasian woman; Donnie and his friend snicker in their seats, watching. "I know we better not see you!"

"It's okay Buddy, we're going to let you slide… again." Officer Jamerson, thick and short in height, gazes at the bulletin board of food and then at the list of food printed upon stacks of colorful flyers. She places her order after Reeds.

"See what I'm talking about? Pa-ra-dise!" Buddy strolls by, whispers then winks at Mel. "I thank you for letting me slide again, my good man and woman friend." Buddy smiles sarcastically, "Now… how's your day been so far, lovely Mrs. Jamerson?"

"Ohh, why don't you answer that one Mr. Reeds, I don't even want to think about it." Jamerson looks at the large bulky man stuffed inside the dark blue and yellow striped police uniform.

"No, no, ladies first, you do the honors." Reeds, not wantin to talk about it either, directs the conversation back on his partner,

"Come on, it couldn't have been that bad, could it?" Not trusting authority, except for in emergencies; Mel, having a thing for pretty women, still manages to give his two cents in the matter.

He wipes his mouth lustfully at the curvature of officer's Jamerson tough physic.

Slowly strutting pass Mel to the counter to wait for their. food, Reeds peer around the store and turns down his shoulder radio. "Set aside from the recent robberies and all the magical deaths popping up, we arrive on the scene last night, not able to leave until this morning. On top of that, we had to explain to four little kids why their uncle and only family member around was going to jail. Buddy, this has to be one of the toughest weeks I've had yet. I've survived gun fights, three days in a row. Had to resolve five gun related incidences yesterday and three today. It's getting bad out here."

"That's terrible." Buddy sticks his hand in his pocket, touching his pre-rolled cigars.

"See what I'm saying? You heard what he said didn't you? Killing after killing, wasn't we talking about that yesterday?" Mel points at Alisha, then at Buddy who waves him off. "It's because of the new gun bill coming out. Their talking about legalizing guns in all states, anybody can get one now, the mentally ill, folks on drugs, kids. That's why you're seeing all these deaths."

"Yeah, where we once use to arrest a person every other day for breaking and entering, now it's like three or four! It's going on everywhere. There are nearly no witnesses to the crimes and most of the properties robbed are occupied by pounds of marijuana plants, entire neighborhoods are like... empty, filled with plants. In every city, state and country, this is happening; ever since they legalized it worldwide, seven years ago." Officer Jamerson shook her head, eyeing the young men in the back, huddling over their food.

"Well like I've always believed, good can't exist without evil. There's always going to be someone who takes a good idea and run it into the ground." Buddy takes their money and opens the register.

"But it shouldn't be at the price of someone's life. There was just a shooting down the street and another one in front of Pete's the other day! It's at least a body, a week now." Jamerson places her hands on her hips and rolls her tired stiff neck in small circular motions.

"It's almost over, it'll be time to go home soon." Officer Reeds sighs as Alisha brings them their sandwiches and drinks. "Buddy, you best be good and careful by what cha doing up in here. Be safe, okay?"

"You don't got to worry about a thing. I got medical reasons and I'm government supplied. Where can I store it? I don't have a choice but to use my house." Buddy shrugs, the officers stop in the middle of the floor. "I'm too legit to quit."

"Buddy... sure." Officer Jamerson holds back her laughter at the old rambling black man.

"See, I was going to leave but since you keep talking so much smack, I'm intrigued now! Show me then." Officer Reeves walks back to the counter. "And if I don't see a permit or medical papers... Buddy... you're going to have to come with us this time."

Buddy looks the policemen in the eye, "I ain't scared." he walks away confidently.

"See, he done wrote a check that he can't cash! His mouth done moved too quick for his own good." Mel whispers to the young men who were now quiet at the table.

Omar, the young African man that worked for Buddy, finishes cleaning the other side of the store. Still with headphones blasting in his ears, he follows Buddy into the basement to retrieve a squeegee for the windows. "Move dummy, when are you going to move that scrap heap that you call a car from in back of the store? It's a fire hazard... and do some real work, boy!" He yells at Omar who just smiles, listening to his loud music. "Get out my way and take off them dang yellow gloves! Why you always got on damn dishwashing gloves?" Buddy takes a silver canister from a pile on the floor and over looks his plump, mature bushes of marijuana plants growing in the corner of the basement. "My babies." He smells the colorful buds. Climbing the wooden stairs, Buddy exits and slams the door behind him with the heel of his foot. "Mel, lock the doors for a second. "Buddy instructs as the two young men, stop eating and lean forward in their seats to see. Buddy walks from behind the register and slams the container on the first table for everyone to see. Prying open the lid, Buddy lifts his paperwork from inside of the tin lid. "I told ya. Here's my papers and this… is my medication." Buddy displays over a hundred pre-rolled joints inside the container. "Miracle Marijuana, I call it, my M&M's."

"Well I'll be. This guy." Officer Reeds removes his hat and looks at his partner.

"Buddy, I can't believe you're showing that. That's a lot, and you got more in the basement? That's crazy!" Alisha returns to the grill after seeing the stash. "I can see it's time to look for a new job." She mutters to herself. "This is too hot for me."

"You must got something awful to be getting this much, I understand?" Reeds looks at Buddy with great concern.

"Yeah Buddy, that's a lot of wacky-Tobacky, What's the problem with you? We've been knowing you for years and you've never told us you were sick or anything." Mel peers at him seriously.

"Well guys, I don't like to talk about my problems much, but I have a terminal cancer and severe arthritis throughout my body." Buddy closes the container and takes it back into the basement.

"Damn it, there's a shooting on 21st street near Maple. That's us, we've got to go!" Reeds overhears the call on his radio. "Let us out would you please, sir? Buddy we have to go! You all take care of yourselves, later!" Reeds yell behind the counter and follows the slow moving old Mel to the door.

"I just got my sandwich!" Officer Jamerson huffs, closing the wrapper on her food. "Buddy, thanks for the food Alisha. Mel." She exits out in a rush.

"They're in pursuit!" Were the last words uttered from officer

Reeds mouth before he and his partner disappear inside their cruiser, driving off.

"That's a hell of a job." Buddy returns to the register blowing cigar smoke from his nose. "Somebodies got to do it."

"Them two never get to sit." Alisha blurts out from the grill.

"Buddy, how long you been sick? I'm your friend, you never told me about a condition." Mel plops his coffee down against the table slightly spilling it.

"I ain't tell nobody but Alisha and Omar, they're enough! Shoot, I don't need everybody worrying about little old me. Hell, I ain't even tell my family." Buddy raises both arms and taps his ashes on the counter.

Omar steps out of the basement, looks around, then pats his pants pockets as if he had forgotten something; disappearing back downstairs.

"Do y'all hear my best friend? Give me that cigar, right now! Gimme that thing!" Mel demands, holding out his shaking hand.

"I'm a grown as man, get out of here! Besides, you know I only smoke on occasions." Buddy argues.

"Yeah, I know, every occasion. Don't you smoke that thing no more!" Mel gets up, walks over and snatches the stogy, dropping it in his cold cup of coffee.

"I hope you drink that too!" Buddy brings laughter to the room as a regular customer named Horace enters the store.

"Buddy." Horace stumbles to the counter and slaps a wad of money into his hands.

"Boy, you still ain't tell her that you're not working, yet?" Buddy tilts his head at the young white man dressed in shirt and tie. "What's wrong with you?"

"No. Hey Alisha, Mel." Horace nervously greets, glancing at the two suspicious young men talking at the back table over empty plates. "Are we good?"

"Yeah." Buddy smacks his dry lips. "Your two knuckle headed friends standing outside are out there every day doing nothing, when are they going to get a job or something? They're making me look bad." Buddy looks out the front window of the store at two men waiting for Horace to return. "Nah… they're cool kids. Now what else do you need, boy? Your little brats were already in here once." Buddy stares at Horace still standing there as if he had something to say.

"Come on, check your hand, you tell me. Why you being so obvious today? I'll wait right here." Horace kept glancing out the windows as if someone was coming; making sure the coast was clear.

"Be right back." Ignoring the nosey eyes of his friends, Buddy sucks his teeth and slowly goes down into the basement.

"I told you, we're gonna get plugged now!" Donnie whispers to his friend, watching enthusiastically. Anxious, they bump knuckles, Donnie smiles deviously over his plate.

"Selling it too, seriously?" Mel looks over at Horace. "So, you still running from the misses, eh? Poor soul you. What you going to do when bill come, wait for her to smack you on the head again? Once a fool, always a fool. Alisha, could you get me another, sweetie?" Mel orders another coffee.

"I got the bill money saved, it's just… what am I going to do when it runs out? We will be needing other things too, you know, and things come up that you don't plan." Horace sits the classified section of the newspapers down upon the counter top. "I've been trying Mel."

"So why you spending all your extra? If she doesn't know, she will real soon." Mel laughs.

"What do you mean by that?" The bell signaling incoming customers, dings. Horace's wife, Keena walks in.

"Those kids!" Keena mumbles as her look of anger changes into a look of surprise. "Horace, what are you doing here… honey? Weren't you supposed to be at work over an hour ago?"

"I, I wanted to grab a bite to eat for later… for, for lunch." Horace stutters, Buddy returns from downstairs.

"But the food counter is back there, why are you over here at the grocery counter? How long have you been waiting for your food, honey?" Keena gazes at him puzzled and looks over at Alisha on the grill not cooking anything.

"Horace, what's up?" Buddy interrupts. Shaking Horace hand, he discreetly inserts a half ounce plastic bag of pre-rolled M-M's into his hand.

"Buddy, what's going on, man?" Horace tries to act natural in front of his wife.

"Oh, hecky-no! Do you think I'm stupid? Horace, really? Are you really doing this with me right here? Do I wear the look of stupidity on my forehead?" Keena eyes began to water as she thinks about how hard they had been struggling just to live. "We're barely paying bills!"

"No babe. Stop, it's not like that. We're cool, I got the …" Keena slaps Horace across the face ending his lie, he holds his head down, embarrassed. "Keena, not here."

"You said you're here for food, but you're at the wrong counter, and Buddy comes out the basement and slips a bag in your hand? Prove me wrong Horace, if I'm really wrong and not seeing what I think I'm seeing… prove me wrong then! Open your hand, let me see what's in it?" Keena steps back, hoping that some magical event would take place and empty her husband's hand before he proved to her that he was indeed lying.

"What… Keena?"

"Horace, open your hand." She orders as the entire room watch in laughter, shame, and disgust.

"You heard the lady, Horace. Man up, working man." Mel hobbles over next to Buddy, with the look of, [I told you so.] written all over his face. Horace reveals the goods in his hand, his wife slaps him again.

"I told you he was selling, I told you!" Donnie taps his friend with his ball cap, they cheer discreetly among each other.

Keena storms away to the refrigerator and returns with

speghetti and a big can of tomato paste. "Buddy, ring this up!" She holds back her anger, hurt and all verbal dialog she normally had everyone in the store. Slamming the box and tall can onto the counter top, she unconsciously elbows Horace, searching for money in her purse. And then, syllables slowly began to seep from her quivering lips. "I don't believe you Horace, what else have you lied about?" Sniffles break into an emotional weep as Alisha connects with her pain and watches helplessly. "Can you believe my husband? Out of all the things we've talked about! Our kids need stuff, you came into the relationship... with a daughter, Horace! I'm trying my best to help you. How are you risking your life this way, wasting our money? Wait, you're not even working are you?"

"Keena?" Horace tries to calm her down, but is overpowered by her screaming voice. "Kee..."

"Don't! I'll talk to you whenever you get home, if you still have a home to go to!" Keena snatches her change, the bag and heads to the door; dimes and pennies drop and cling across the floor at her feet. "This may be your last night." Keena stomps to the door.

"Keena, wait!" Horace steps after her.

"Buddy, uh... we're next!" Donnie's friend, the tall guy with an afro, stands up next to him. "We've seen it and we know you got it, now!"

"Boy, if y'all don't sit down or get out of here... ain't nobody contributing to your juvenile habits!" Buddy, waves them off and points to the door.

"Well, one things for sure, we ain't no juveniles and damn sure ain't trying to buy." Donnie's friend places a bandana over his mouth and nose. He pulls a pistol from out the back of his pants. "Sorry, no witnesses." He screws a silencer on the tip of his gun.

"Now you boys wait a second!" Buddy tries to explain as Keena turns back around inside the doorway towards Horace and the sudden commotion.

With his semi-automatic weapon drawn, Donnie shoots

Horace in the neck; Keena screams inside the entrance way. The store fills with flashes of light, gun fire and splatters of blood upon the inside windows. Keena's body fall inside the doorway as the front door gently closes on her leg. The violence ends, two young men, and another, of African dissent and blasting a small radio on his ears, quickly load crates of Buddy's silver canisters onto an old, rusty truck parked near the back of the store. Tossing a gun in back of the truck, smacking its tail light, Omar signals Donnie to drive off to their pre-planned destination.

"But before we discuss the current legislation to legalize guns in America and the current rise in crime, a quick word from our sponser, Rent-A-Weed!" The news anchor on the radio announces on Omars headset as he takes off his yellow, dishwasher gloves and tosses them into the fire set behind the store. "Welcome to the last days, Paradise." Omar smirks, disappearing down the backstreet of thick smoke into an uncertain future, never to be seen again.

The End

THE 11TH LANDING

THE SMOKER

Behind a stubby vibrating Adam's apple, loud gulps of draining liquid turn nearby heads, followed by a harsh thump of a thick glass mug being sat upon a wooden table. Halfway done with his coffee and partially done with his second cigarette, John Banson; tired and beat, strokes his long fingers through his sweating, short cut, wavy brown hair. Taking a couple of semi striding sips from his mug, he catches the fire on his cig, exhaling a cloud of smoke into the cloudless sky.

"Still smoking that stuff, eh John?" A woman, an old co-worker he hadn't seen in a while stroll by. "Those things a kill ya." She continues on her way to the parking lot.

"Life will kill you!" John shouts back, laughing, watching the last remaining employees extinguish their smokes and head for their assigned time clocks. He glances at the clock that hung along the outside wall of the smoke areas of the Post Office. "Does that thing ever work? Why are breaks so short? Oh well, it's over." Glimpsing down at the watch on his arm, straying behind the others, John draws from his cigarette one last time... again, and then one more time for good measures. Indulging in every second of the grayish, white bliss, he is trapped in deep thought, swept under and lost in the cloud of second hand smoke. Glad to be going home, he disperses from the now dissipating mist that is caught by the passing wind. Blowing out his last gust, John is caught by that old too familiar feeling deep inside him... the smokers cough. Choking, he realize he was now standing inside of his workplace with the cigarette butt freshly lit.

"John, again? This is the second time I had to speak you today; now handle it, put it out!" Mr. Hunnington, the tour supervisor harps. Caught off guard, John fumbles the butt in his hands nervously and defuses the small burning cotton on his thumb. His boss turns away agitatedly, and carries on his business.

"John you should know better!" Smiles the warm, yet sexy and equally dark haired electronic technician, Betty. Fortyish and very well maintained, she was one out of the few women that John thought was good looking on his floor.

"My mind must be slipping! I don't know what I was thinking." John shrugs his broad, thin shoulders, slightly embarrassed. In straight leg, fitting jeans and a button up shirt, he slides both hands in his tight pockets and eases by her, to the closest time clock. Coughing twice, John clears his burning throat and rubs his chest.

"See, sounds like they're finally getting to you John, the smoking? Maybe you should put them down? It's not hard, I did it." Old Benson, a very friendly and ready to retire, maintenance worker, struts over pushing a portable garbage bin. "Don't you know those things will kill you?"

"Life will kill you, Benson." John pulls out a white and black magnetic striped time card from his pocket. "You know what... listen." He holds the card up in the air. "Look guys, I'm off the clock. Not even the ALMIGHTY FATHER himself could stop me from smoking! It's my choice, and I say... smoke em if you got em!" John laughs off the words of his friend and swipes his card across the time clock with force. "I'm on fire! Hot!" John skips away.

Heading home, John drives the freeway listening to his favorite songs happily and worry free. An anti-smoking commercial comes on the radio, tempting him to light another needed, yet unneeded jig. John snickers and quickly turns the radio to the oldies station.

Firing up a fresh cancer stick, he relaxes once more inside the quaint personal space of his car. "Yeah, I'm on fire, heh, heh! Smoking! Yeah, I'm on fire... yeah, smoking!" John sings. An automobile just a lane over, unsuspectingly cuts in front of him causing John to slightly serve, avoiding the collision. Cursing at the vehicle, he rolls down the window and waves a fist in the air. Proceeding on, Johns eyes began to water and burn as he starts to fan away a blinding smoke suddenly collecting around him. A flickering light from a small fire that burned somewhere beneath his seat startles him. Touching his lips, "Damn it!" John notices his missing cigarette has dropped somewhere in the car. "Fire, I'm really on fire! Smoking!" He screams, pulling over and hoping out the car. With the door open, John sticks his head into the car and finds the small blaze ignited along the dry carpet and loose trash on the floor. Unable to douse the rapidly growing flames, John gives in; the entire car is swiftly engulfed in fire. Jogging a few feet, yelling for help, John tries to warn the passing traffic not to drive too close. "Fire, my... my cars on fire! Go around, help, call the fire department!" He scans the area for a pay phone, an oncoming motorist, using a cell, ignores him and drives on pass. Not seeing a phone booth or a store in sight, John stops and thinks. He reaches into his pocket and pulls out a full pack of Menthol Lites. Tapping the soft box in the palm of his hand, a single cig slides out. John raises the carton up to his mouth and pulls the cigarette out into the corner cut of his lips. Passing cars blow their horns passing as John walks through traffic head down, sad at his misfortunes. Patting his body for a lighter, John pulls out a trusty, small, green Bic from his pocket. Flicking the lighter twice, John inhales and exhales in relief and great calm. Proud of not losing his cool, his vehicle explodes in the road in a loud bang behind him.

Eventually reaching home; escorted to his apartment building by the city's finest local police department, John wearily carries three citations and a small plastic bag of smoking items that survived. Thanking the officers for the lift, John feels his pockets, discovering his smokes were missing. He bums one off the officer. "Appreciate it." John nods the policemen farewell and slams the door in protest of the tickets and fines. As the police car drives off, John lights the white stick, hitting it hard and deeply; he slowly enters his building. In a plume of smoke, John slowly makes his way up the hall stairs to the upper floor. Upon the second level, he lifts the cigarette to take another puff. Bumping his hand on the railing, the cig flips loose from his fingers, disappearing over the banister. "Really, are you kidding me?" John sighs as a nice looking young woman switches down the stairs towards him. "Hi, hello... how are you today?" He quickly straightens up and attempts to greet the highly attractive woman as sincerely as possible. The smiling woman face drops and her nose crinkles up upon contact with the smell of strong cigarettes that emitted from his body. Receiving no reply as the woman steps by, John blows his breathe into his hands and smells them; his head jerks back in disgust. "Ugh, I see."

Reaching the third floor, John heads for the door numbered 301. "Damn it!" He steps to the door, remembering that his keys were left in the ignition of the exploding car. Dropping his head, barely touching the silver door knob, the handle falls apart, dropping screws and rings across the toe of his shoe. "What?" John's index finger gently touches the door; completely pushing it open. Revealing a tattered living room and a kitchen in shambles, the apartment displays a bedroom which blossomed of utter destruction; indicating an intruder had broken in. John Banson, stood in amazement at the mess he had to clean; shocked by how someone could just come in and ransack his home. Owning nothing of real value, John was sure that nothing was stolen. Within minutes, down upon a small lamp stand, he eyes a box of cigarettes. Lifting the light, hard box to eye level, John quickly discovers that there is only one left. Slightly tilting and shaking the container, John nudges the smoky treat out of the box; it falls between his dry lips. Feeling for a lighter, he magically scoops one up from the floor. Lighting the paper end of the tobacco stuffed square, John inhales deeply and leans backwards against his couch that was for some reason, flipped upside down. Blowing a thick smog of a white, cancerous, haze into the room, John finds the TV remote onside the couch and presses the power button to the television. Receiving no response, lazily without looking, John aims the remote in different angles trying to catch a signal. Pressing the volume and mute button, he checks the remote for damage and batteries. Becoming frustrated, John tiresomely swings his body around and points the remote at his television which was missing from his home. "Great, burglarized." He sighs, instantly drifting into a slight depression.

"Oh my goodness John, are you alright? Do you need the police?" Clara Smertz, the next door neighbor, stood in the doorway behind him with her arms crossed. Startling John, he falls off the corner of the couch and stands.

"This is terrible! Are you okay John? Were you here when they came in? How's your head?" An old, crackly, high pitched voice rambles on around him as Mrs. Cambell, the sweet yet sour, nosey old woman from across the hall steps from behind Clara.

Slightly in a love struck daze, stuck between another beautiful face and the tragedy of his apartment, John stares into bright blue eyes as soft hands are placed upon his cheeks; the wrinkled face of Mrs. Cambell comes into view. "Mrs. Cambell, Clara... you girls scared me a little." John places one hand over his heart and continues his square with the other. "I'm okay Mrs. Cambell, thanks for being concerned. They broke through my front door and stole my set. I sure wish I would have been here, I could have stopped them!" John smacks his knee.

"Now don't you go wishing things you might regret, you could have gotten hurt. Or... worst yet, they could have been kids, you just never know. They're killing nowadays, John." Clara interrupts him. "Did they steal any money?"

"I don't know, so far, just my television. I haven't really went through the other rooms or anything. I don't care anymore, look at this place. Look at the mess I have to clean." John gripes, kicking his belongings sadly from out in front of him. "My car blew up today, they fined me. What's next, you know?"

"Blew up? Well, you're just having all sorts of bad luck today aren't you? Poor dear, I'm sorry to hear that, John." Mrs. Cambell shakes her head, looking around at all the furniture turned over in the apartment.

"I don't know what to do right now?" John looks over at the two women looking up at him with watery eyes. "Ladies, I... I'm sorry. I don't mean to vent and put my burdens on you. You've caught me at a bad time right now." Quite embarrassed and sad, John gently shoves them by the waist and backwards towards the door, gently guiding them out.

"You, you need to do something about this! File a report with the police or something? I can help you! Don't you want your things returned, John?" Cries Mrs. Cambell, tripping over clothes pencils. Watching the front door draw nearer, the old woman realizes John was putting them out. "John?"

"John, how long have I've known you? Listen," Clara is pushed out into the hall, "John? I can't believe your acting this way, we just came to help!" She stares at him with those clear hazel bedroom eyes. Puckering her soft plump lips; John closes the door in Clara's face.

"I can't with them, not today." John presses his back against the door, keeping them from coming in. As they pound on the door several times, John eyes his now broken cigarette by the corner of the door. Bending down, lighting it, he listens to the women outside in the hall.

"We can hear you smoking Johnny, those things aren't going to help you! You need to save money now and quit! Let us in John!" The old woman insist as Clara roll her eyes and opens the door to her apartment.

"Maybe good things will happen to him when he stops shoving people around him away!" Frowning, Clara goes inside her apartment and slams the door.

"Well, goodbye John, I'll be right across the hall if you need anything. Things will get better, you just wait and see… and stop smoking while you're still young! Those things will kill you." Mrs. Cambell shakes her head and quietly hobbles back across the hall to her apartment.

"Demon, the lies! Goodbye Mrs. Cambell!" John shouts and peers down at his cigarette. "Never, this is the only pleasure I got! It's life that kills ya!" He shouts into his empty living room. "You may have taken my car and my TV…. but no human, animal, thing or GOD can come between a man and his smokes. No one!" John relights the cig and inhales the small remaining end until the cotton start to sizzle. "I've got to find my packs." He mumbles, tossing the butt down on his tan carpet, stomping it out. Standing tall, facing the task at hand, John sighs and begin to slowly restore his apartment back to its original state. Fixing everything close to how it was, hours later, John finds himself underneath the cool sheets of his cozy bed. Having also discovered that not only had his television been stolen, but his stereo and laptop had been taken as well, John pulls out another cigarette he found, and stuffs it casually in the corner of his mouth. Needing a lighter, he gets up and lights from the top burner of the stove. Returning to the softness of his mattress, John blows a few slowly expanding zero shaped clouds underneath the ceiling. "Quit smoking, hmph. Why? We all could die right now, at any given time anyway." John puts out the cig and closes his eyes. "Me, quit, nah… I'm not a quitter." He laughs to himself and gradually dozes off.

The next morning John awakens with a breath of new life and hope, nothing would stop him from having a good day. Rising from the maroon sheets of the soft cushioned king sized bed, John stand up and stretches, smiling at the sight of small birds playfully flying about his window. Feeling his shirt pocket, he pulls out the cig from last night and retrieves something from under the sheets that had been poking him all night; a lighter. Flicking it twice, he watches a bird poop on his window before gleefully gliding away. "Good luck." John shrugs his shoulders, blowing out another cloud. With a smile, he leaps to bathroom to do his morning, hygienic duties. Coming out refreshed and revived, John proceeds to breakfast. Mouthwatering, the last five stripes of bacon commenced to sizzle as a second skillet was found to scramble the eggs. Pulling the last three eggs out the refrigerator, John, holding a cigarette in his mouth, was reminded yet again, that it was probably a good idea to plan on going grocery shopping soon. Taking a quick draw, the cig burns to the cotton as the heat intensifies, singeing John's lip. "Ow!" He drops the butt into the pan of hot frying bacon, splashing grease around the top of the oven. A small fire emerges from under the skillet, Johns three delicate eggs, roll from his hand, splattering at his feet. Tossing the blazing pan in the sink, he turns on the faucet, drowning each and every crispy strip of bacon. "Dang it." John stares down at the puddle of raw egg, disappointingly. Within the hour, John was continuing on with his beautiful new day at the kitchen table, eating soggy bacon and gritty, shelled, scrambled eggs.

Apologizing for his actions on the previous day, John voluntarily takes out Clara's and Mrs. Cambell's garbage as a peace treaty between them. Successfully placing the trash in their proper aluminum cans, John walks to the bus stop. Heading for work, he smiles at the beautiful sky beneath the warming Sun and walks away from his apartment with high aspirations. Lighting a cig, John takes a long pull; behind him, a small cat leaps out to forage, the feline knocks over Clara's and Mrs. Cambell's garbage cans. "This is going to be a good day." John smiles like an android, reminding himself over and over again how great the day would be. Devotedly arriving at his job early, John notices his stomach beginning to bubble. Breaking into a deep sweat, he runs pass other employee's, breaking into the bathroom.

Searching for an empty stall, he falls to one knee before the porcelain throne. Buckled over, stomach tightening, John receives a fainting sensation. Having been sick before, he knew this time, something was different and very wrong. Growing extremely dehydrated and mouth dry, a mist of smoke began to ooze from Johns throat. "GOD, I'll never eat off the floor again!" John jerks back holding his neck. "What's happening to me? I don't feel so... good." He lunges back over the bowel; ounces of tobacco pour from his mouth. Gagging and choking up a few more cup fulls, John slides back to the wall, covering his mouth in shock. Awed by what was happening, he eases back towards the edge of the bowl. Peeking down into the water, he flushes the toilet at the sight of the floating tobacco. "What was that? How? This can't be real!" John checks the temperature of his forehead with his hand. Not knowing what to say or do, John does what he do best; he checks his pockets for smokes and a lighter. Finding only his lighter, he suddenly feels something crawl up his throat and into his mouth. Slightly gagging, John pushes out a long menthol cigarette from between his lips with his tongue and unconsciously lights its end. "Wait...what?" He spits the cigarette onto the tile floor. "Where'd that come from? Oh my GOD, what's happening to me? Okay, someone's playing a trick on me... no, no, no... maybe... I'm still asleep?" John plucks out a string of his own hair and races to the sink to look in the mirror. Turning on the faucet, John fills his hands with cold water. Closing his eyes, he splashes his face with several dozens of cigarettes. "Who threw those?" John shouts, peering around the empty bathroom. "This is a joke isn't it? Some ones playing a big trick on ol Johnny boy today, humph? Very funny, okay, okay, who's the bad magician? Come on out, you're terribly not funny!" John puts his ear low to the floor and checks beneath all the stalls, finding himself alone in the bathroom. "I must be going crazy." John tells himself, staring into an empty stall. "Pull yourself together John, your hallucinating." He repeats in his mind. "Must be the stress?"

Slowly strolling back to the sink, John looks in the mirror and takes a deep breath. Refilling his hands with cold water, John raises his h2o filled palms, closes his eyes before the splash and douses his face and neck with hundreds of menthol-lite cigarettes. Drawing back in fright, John hears and sees the small and slender sticks dropping to the floor. In a shuttering yelp, he runs out the bathroom in horror. Nervously passing postal employees that he didn't directly work with, John speed walks to the time clock and clocks in early for work. Calming his nerves, John struts to the daily productivity board and skims through the production scores, goals and work schedule. Seeing what mail sorting machine he was scheduled to be on that day, he walks to his assigned sorter. Setting up equipment, he checks the computer of the sorter to make sure the right program was inputted. With everything in place, including the trays of mail he was running, John clears his mind of the strange occurrences of the day and starts the two man operation by himself. Grabbing a foot long tray of perfectly straight mail, John flips it onto a narrow vibrating, mail jogging ledge on the loading end of the machine. As the jogger loosens and straightens the letters to be ran, John slides over another flipped tray of mail and connects it to the previously loaded row of letters. Feeding the mail into the sorter, the machine reads thousands of letters in minutes, sorting them to their proper bins along the machine.

A red light flashes on the mail sorter indicating… "A jam." John hears the sorter stop and buzzers sound off. All too familiar with the all-day ritual of clearing frequent jams out the machine, John restarts the sorter in hopes the jam will clear itself. As the sorter stops again, its light flickers and buzzers sound further down the forty foot long machine. John starts the machine several more times; slowly feeding mail onto the ledge of its loading belt. Noticing an unusual rattle and a poof of shredded paper dust, John hits the emergency stop button. The machine comes to an instant halt; a dozen of jam lights flash on the tops of various sections of the machine as John decides to manually clear them. Seeing nothing in the transparent section of the machine that takes pictures of the mail, he blows dust from around the lens of the computers eye and closes its cover. Finding nothing in the rows and columns of bins called {Stackers}, in which the letters push out of and stacked in, John walks to the end of the sorter, to the reject bin. He pulls out a broken rubber belt that was clogging and burning the mail. Apparently it had snapped off of one of the small rollers inside the machine and caused the malfunction. Looking down at the twisted and bent mail stuffed in the stacker, John pulls back the plastic flap that holds the mail in place to straighten the letters. Extracting a hand full of mail, thousands of cigarettes equivalent to the amount of mail he ran, erupts from the hold out. "What... the? Hey!" Dodging the rain of Rollies, John flees back to the front of his machine. Nervously picking up letters from the row mail laid over on the ledge, John watches the envelopes crumple into cigarettes right before his eyes, slipping and falling between his fingers onto the floor. Totally dumbfounded, John leans against the sorter nervously biting his nails. "Okay John, what is going on? What is going on? This is not real." Trembling, scared and confused, he places one hand on top of the row of mail still loaded on the sorters ledge, over fifty pieces of mail crumple into small, white, cigarettes. Quite jittery, John scans the area to make sure no one was watching the mess he was creating and sees Mr. Hunnington (The boss) swiftly approaching the sorter. Sweeping the loading ledge clear of cigs, John quickly sweeps the ones in front of the machine away with his foot.

"Banson? John Banson, what on earth are you doing here so early? It's not your shift. Are you on unauthorized overtime, because I certainly don't remember you being on the overtime list?" Mr. Hunnington speaks loudly while fumbling through his clip board of papers. His face steams angrily with red and neck swells with veins.

"Um, I, I, I.. know. I mean no! I was dropped off hours ago so instead of sitting here twiddling my thumbs, I thought I'd be productive and get us some numbers today. Since I was already here." John comes up with a fast excuse. Stepping up close to Mr. Hunnington, John tries to divert his attention from the mess around the machine. Quickly spinning around, John starts the machine, frantically pushing the remaining mail through the feeder; the sorter discreetly sucks in cigarettes.

"I got my eye on you John, and why does it smell like tobacco over here? Have you been smoking on my floor again? Do you want me to lose my job, John?" Mr. Hunnington's balding head shines a bright glow upon his dark skin, his thick eyebrows lower, covering both beady eyes. He and John both peer down at the loose cigarettes surrounding the base of the mail sorter.

"I can explain… It wasn't me, when…" John turns back around to explain as more cigarettes sling from his clothing.

"John Banson, what is the meaning of this? Again?" The heavy set, elderly man's body seemed to expand like a cobra before striking. "You, you've been smoking on the floor?"

"No, no sir, I haven't been! You wouldn't believe what's been going on today!" John holds out both hands beginning to plead his case as lit mentholated cigarettes protrude from between every one of his fingers.

"Unbelievable! The nerve! I don't know what kind of ship you think I'm running but, I'm not in the mood for your games, John! You're fired Banson! You have five minutes to remove yourself from my floor! Clock out and turn in your card." Mr. Hunnington storms away as John slumps over the machine. Cigarettes fall from the jogger ledge like droplets of rain on top of his shoes.

"This… is… unbelievable." Gripes John before picking himself up and moping to the time clock to punch out for good. As cigarettes tumble from his pockets and pants legs, John leaves a long broken trail of smokes behind. Ignoring the cold stares and stopping cars, John snaps his fingers, igniting a cig the magically appears between his thumb and pointer finger. Placing it in his mouth, he sucks down a breath of smoke. Exhaling, John feels a little light headed and dizzy as he now holds twelve blazing cigarettes in between his lips. Spitting the sticks out onto the ground, he gasps for air. "Too much, too much smoke! I need to get home." John darts away from the building towards the street, pass old Benson who drives by slowly in his car.

"Not your brand, eh John?" Mr. Benson laughs and continues on his way to work.

"Now's not the time Mr. B!" John passes a bus stop of postal workers and a hand full of people, angrily. Spotting a man puffing heavenly, enjoying his smoke, John grits his teeth and holds up a hand of lit cigarettes well balanced upon his fingertips. "They're not that great!" He leaves the people puzzled at the bus stop. Jogging pass a pay phone, John runs back to make a call to his friend, Clara Smertz; he needed someone who'd believe his story to talk too. The phone rings several times; John bites his nails on his left hand to nubs. Anxiously awaiting to share his problem with the only person he was currently close too, a calm dainty voice answers the other end.

"Hello?" Clara greets a second time.

"Clara its John, can you talk? We need to talk!" John huffs heavily.

"John, is that you? Why are you breathing so hard? Why do you sound so far away?" Were her last words before the phone disconnects.

"Wha... I'm not... Clara? Hello, hello?" John digs deep into his pockets, finding another fifty cents. Nearly depositing the coins into the coin slot of the pay phone, John face melts into a sick expression as both quarters transform into cigarettes before entering the coin slot. "Hey, no! How? No, the first ones took, aww come on!" John tries to insert more coins as they all fall to the ground as cigarettes. Feeling cursed and alienated, John finds himself knocking desperately at Clara's door, cigarettes fly from his shirt sleeve in every which direction. Getting no response, John places his ear upon the door and listens for any sign of life. Hearing the low vocal tones of a man and woman, a slight hint of jealousy touches Johns spirit as he envisions Clara (of whom he cares a great deal for but never voiced his true feelings to) seeing another man. "I can hear you two in there you know?" John yells into the corner of the door as sweet sounds of love making chokes his swallow. "The heck, really? How could she? She was just over my house!" His mouth drops as sounds of a woman being well pleased pierce his soul and the thought of her with another man rip at the back of his mind. Having known Clara for years and never once telling her about his true feelings towards her, Johns confused facial expression twist and bend into a mad, angry face. He kicks Clara's door clean open. "Clara, I love you!" John barges in the apartment proclaiming his love to her television set left on.

"John?" Clara's pleasant voice calls out from behind. "What are you doing here and how'd you get in?"

"Clara?" John sneers at a love movie playing on the set. "Uhhhhh…" He searches his brain for the right words to say.

"My door?" She rushes in dropping a cake pan. "The door is knocked right off the hinge! John, what are you doing in my house? Did you do this?"

"Clara, I'm sorry but I needed to tell you something, something about you and me, us. Please, listen?" John holds his hands together in a praying manor.

"Now you listen! You shut me out yesterday, John. You put me out of your house and everything. All I wanted was to know if you were okay, to be there for you! Now today, you kick in my door and your excuse is that you want to talk?" Clara gazes at him with hurt and daggers in her eyes. "Are you on drugs, how does that sound? John, leave now, before I call the cops!"

"What… why? No Clara, it's not like that, please…. listen! Don't call the police."

"Why shouldn't I, why not? Give me a good reason. I mean…

why should I listen to you today? You didn't want to hear me at all yesterday! So, your apartment was broken into and now you've broken into mine? Are we even or something now? Or maybe it was a lie; maybe you made it look like somebody broke into your apartment so no one would know that you were really breaking into everyone else's!" Clara steps back as thoughts and mixed emotions flood her mind, clouding her judgment.

"Look, I know how this looks but please, you have to trust me! Clara..." John reaches for her hand as she pulls away from him. "I don't know how to explain this but, I thought you were in here with someone else and I accidentally kicked the door in. I guess, I was a little jealous, I never got a chance to tell you how I truly felt about you Clara." John tries to explain; actually digging a deeper hole for himself.

"So because you thought another man was in my house that gives you the right to break in? I got news for you John, we're not together, and never been. I don't think so mister! John, you have completely lost it! You are officially crazy." Clara picks up the land line house phone and begins dialing the authorities. "I've heard enough."

"Clara no, wait! I need your help! I have nowhere else to go and no one to turn too." John's words grab her attention for just a second; Clara pauses in the middle of dialing 9-1-1. "I, I do want to be with you Clara, I've always wanted to be with you. Sorry for the door. I promise I'll pay for it."

"What?" Clara stands confused, with a blank look on her face. Holding the phone, John's words begin to slightly touch her. "John, you're crazy."

Picturing himself losing her, John decides now was the time to tell her. "Clara I know this may look and sound weird and all, but I really do enjoy your company and I've been waiting for the right time to tell you how I've felt about you for the longest. Probably too long. I'm going through something right now and I really, really need you." John gazes into her wide oval eyes.

"And this is how you tell me? Out of all this time... it took for you to be caught red handed, breaking and entering for you to tell me how you feel? Now... out of all the times I've begged you to go out with me, you expect me to believe some mystical small part of you now wants to be with me?" Clara drifts back to her senses. "What do you take me for, a fool, John?" She hangs up the phone and gets another dial tone.

"Clara, no. I'm not Lying to you, I didn't come to your apartment to break in. It was a mistake; this is just a misunderstanding! I came for you." John crosses his fingers behind his back in hopes she would listen as cigarettes randomly drop from his sleeves. "I was having a bad day, I was angry... I thought I had missed my last chance at telling you how I felt. I thought some fantastic guy was in here winning you over."

"Out of all this time, now?" Clara looks up at the ceiling and shakes her head. Hanging up the phone, she looks down by his feet. "And look... you promised to quit smoking a long time ago... that's a problem for me too, John. I want to live a smoke free life in a smoke free environment. You still live to smoke. How can you say you want me and you're still putting your habits ahead of what's important to me? Your life, ha! How am I to deal with that John? We can't grow old together at the rate you're smoking?" Clara makes perfect sense; John tries to cover the cigarettes she hasn't seen with his foot.

"But that's what I'm trying to tell you, for you... I can stop!" John crosses his toes inside his shoes, "These cigarettes aren't even mine! I mean... they are but... I don't smoke them." John tries his best to explain his new unknown condition. Closing his hands together; a blast of cigarettes fly at Clara's face. As she screams, cigarettes leak from his shirt and pour from his pants legs. "Seriously?" John sees all his efforts of getting with Clara, going down the drain. "See, this is what I'm talking about... sorry!" He flings more cigarettes over her head, trying to apologize. Wiping his mouth, ten cigs magically align John's lips. With no explanation for the explosion of smokes from his body, John glimpse at Clara with watery eyes; dashing away in embarrassment. "I'm going to pay for the door... and get you a maid!" John passes his apartment, runs down the stairs and back outside. Sprinting, running from life and his problems, John dashes for answers in a wind of flying cigarettes. Feeling as close to an abomination to mankind as one possibly could, the fired postal worker take shelter in a local bar and sulks deep into a chair with his problems. Ordering to ease his mind, John finds a clever way to drink from glasses without really touching them. Feeling extremely freakish, mad at GOD and disappointed at himself, John glares down into a glass of his third shot of liquor. A cigarette lights between two of his fingers; he stares into his own reflection, then sadly upon the condensation on the glass. "Ouch!" John pokes himself in the eye with the cigarette, still taking a tote. Scooting the glass close to the edge of the table, he shoves the shot glass over with his arm, holds his head down by the rim of the table, skillfully spilling liquor into his mouth, onto his shirt, pants and floor, as a familiar voice speaks into his ear.

"Can I bum one off ya?" Old Mr. Benson walks over and pats John on the back twice, sitting down next to him.

"Mr. B, you don't smoke." John, barely able to form a smile, laughs sorrowfully with tears in his eyes. Folding his arms and propping his head down upon them like a tired hound, John tilts his head, and looks over at his ex-fellow coworker before gazing across the room. John thinks of the good paying job he once had and what his future will become.

"Ah, you remember?" Mr. Benson laughs, "I tell the truth, but occasionally I like to look like a politician." The friendly old man smiles a set of gapped teeth.

"Here you go, pick one." John holds up four fingers which securely held three lit cigarettes between every two.

"Mr. Benson takes one and watches John close his hand and drop it to his side as if there weren't eight burning cigarettes inside his palm. "I say, that's a mighty fine trick you do there. I know a lot of men who'd pay a lot to learn a skill like that. You would turn heads at a party that's for sure." Mr. Benson slides a hot cup of Joe on the table top.

"Well like you always said Mr. B, smoking will kill you. That's just one trick I'd really like to unlearn. I'd pay just to be my old self again." John sighs and grit his teeth until his jaw bones could be seen moving along the corners of his face.

"Be yourself again? My goodness, John! Well, if your life has changed that drastically is sounds to me as though you only have one way to get it back? Oh shoot… I almost forgot, John, you can't smoke in public places anymore." The old man puts out the cig on the sole of his shoe. "Thanks for the smoke, now if you'd excuse me John; I must go to the gentlemen's room. Talk to HIM, John." Mr. Benson leaves his coffee and cigarette on the table and heads to the bathroom. The bartender makes his way to John's direction.

Distraught, not even noticing the old man leaving, John sits with his head down holding a smoking cig.

"Hey buddy, you're going to have to put that out!" The bartenders deep, loud voice, renders over the bar, stretching to Johns table. Interrupting John's blank thoughts, the bartender watches him put out his smoke and returns to serving customers.

Not ready to sober up but deciding it's probably best, John takes his shot to the head and heads to the bar for a coffee. Tilting the shot glass down, John notices another cigarette burning between each of his dark, yellow fingers.

"Hey, you can't smoke in here!" The bartender belched from behind the bar counter. The sound of his voice smacks John in the face, causing him to spill the glass of beer. As the brown alcohol touch his hands, cigarettes spread across the countertop.

"Sorry, I forgot… sorry!" John swiftly swipes the bar clean with his arm and shoves his hands in his pockets. "Coffee please, black." He wipes his face with his sleeve as the bartender places a mug of cream-less dark coffee, in front of him. Nervously grinning at the muscle bound man, John peers down at his reflection in the black, contents of the glass. Appearing to be smoking five cigarettes, John's reflection winks, sending him jumping back, away from the bartender who looks at him curiously. Spitting out the cigarettes, John notices that he is surrounded by a small audience of locals. Majority male and a few women, John figured some of the gathered were bartenders and bouncers of the bar according to the size of their necks. Swiveling around, John looks down at two rows of smoking cigarettes, perfectly balanced on the toes of both of his gym shoes. The women step back fascinated; John shrugs his shoulders, holding up two arms and wrist aligned with cigarettes. Quickly stuffing his hands back into his pockets, both of John's pants legs ignite with flames; the male bartender douses the fire out with two pitchers of hot coffee. In a scalding cry, John darts off in a cloud of smoke and cigarettes, humorously petrifying anyone who caught a glimpse of him.

The skies churn of a gloomy gray, over the cool sprinkles of moderate rain that fell across the city and upon Johns head. Shivering down an alley, John falls to his knees; beads of rain dripping from his soaked hair and clothing. "I'm Cursed! Why have you cursed me?" He cries out to the heavens, sitting in the middle of a puddle of floating cigs. "Why me? Why are you doing this, what did I do to deserve this?" John looks up at the dark sky. "As if my life didn't already suck! First, my apartment was violated, then my job, which I lost for good because of you! They already didn't like me! Not to mention... because of you, I've fumbled it up with the most fantastic and beautiful woman on the planet! No woman's ever interested in me... but her! One..." John yells at the sky, shouting until he was out of breath, "and I messed that up. Why GOD, why are you punishing me?" John thinks about Mr. Bensons words. "Look, I know I don't talk to you much. I'M sorry for whatever I did. I just want my life back. I know that I haven't been totally loyal to your laws but I can't do this without you. Father, I'm praying to you now, please, lift this curse. I beg of you! Only you can help me, I'm sorry for everything. I repent, I repent my sins!" John prays, wishing, believing that his life could change. Hoping, eyes closed tight; John slowly opens them, stands and looks around to see if anyone was watching. Eyeing a small kitten, curled under a bench, John watches the feline quiver and shake in the cold rain just as he was. Thinking of his life, Clara and funny old Mr. Benson, John hears talking. Listening, he makes out the chatter to be a group of men arguing.

"No more excuses Bobby, stop running from us, this is the end of the line!" A loud shout blares through the holes of a wooden fence. "Where is it?"

"But I told you! I have no idea of what you're talking about! Now stop hitting me… please! I swear, I don't know, I don't know anything!" A smaller, more whining sounding man inches backwards, just enough for John to see the back of him. "Just leave me alone, geesh!"

"No more lies Bob, it's over. The only thing that can save you now is an act of GOD, and HE ain't here right now!" Another voice, even heavier than the first, echo throughout the alley. "Check his pockets."

"I told you before, I don't have any money! You leave my wife and daughter out of it!" The smaller voice pleads as John receives a funny feeling inside. Biting his lip, clinching his hands into fist, Heart beating against his chest loudly, John knew he had to do something. Not seeing any other witnesses or the police, John had to act fast to save whoever was on the other side of that fence from the brutes. Hurrying to the corning of the fence, scared, John spots two men dressed in leather jackets and jeans confronting a very short and balding man in a suit. A cigarette appears between John's index and middle finger. One of the men, wearing sunglasses, pulls out a gun and aims it at the little man; the tip of John's square ignites. "I'll show you Almighty." John charges the men, flinging cigarettes out from his hands. Instantly, a wall of tobacco and cigarettes collect and swell behind the two men, tidal waving over them. "Wow." John looks down at the mess he just somehow created. "Run little guy!" He yells to the man as the sound of a gun goes off. Eyeing the old man fall, clutching his stomach, John eyes the two men rise to their feet, now, coming after him. "They have guns, they have guns!" John dashes in the opposite direction as a tornado of cigarettes whip from his body and lashes upon the men chasing him. Between buildings, short cutting through hallways, back onto the far off streets, John disappears into the city underneath a haze of light rain.

"Cut, cut, cut, who was that?" The director of a small low budget film, helps his three friends up from a debris of wet cigarettes. "Who's going to clean this up?"

"I dunno but he messed up the whole shot! The scene is ruined. Idiot!" The largest man in sunglasses picks up his prop gun from the ground.

"I thought he was a surprise addition to the scene, he had some great special effects! Who hired that guy?" The old man who played as Bobby in the film, stood and dusted off his costume. Peering at the approaching camera crew and the overwhelming piles of cigarettes, he stands with the film crew, baffled by what just happened.

The next morning, John opens his eyes to the sight of a small, nearly weightless, red bird perched upon his forehead. The robin whistles, John blinks as it flies away. Sitting up, refreshed and drenched along a bus stop bench on his street, John, feeling the same, yet different, snaps his fingers and looks down at his hands and feet. Noticing absolutely no cigarettes around him and not even sure of how he even acquired the strange abilities in the first place, John smiles thankfully, and takes his first step of the day towards home. Humbled at life, and thankful for a second chance, John Banson, feeling blessed, holds his head high, embracing the fresh air of the new morning. Stopping at local corner store, John picks up a few things along the way. Then, finally home, he takes a soothing hot bath, followed by a long awaited, delicious, hot breakfast that he happily prepared and enjoyed. Resting his mind, regrouping his thoughts on the couch, John comes across an apology note from Clara pinned to the armrest. Reading it, John smiles happily at his broken door. Clara had invited him to dinner, a movie and an overnight stay at her apartment for the weekend. "Thank you, you're the man!" John cheers, pointing to the heavens beyond the ceiling. Going to need money for his date, John decides to go to his old job and pick up his last check.

Even though he never really enjoyed his job and dealt with a lot of stress, it was indeed a job he felt lucky to have had the opportunity to work for. After all, it did pay his bills and helped him to save money. Inside of personnel at the United States Postal service, John shows the security his declined postal I.D. Mr. Hunnington, his old boss, enters the room.

"Ah John, just the person I wanted to see." Mr. Hunnington walks up next to his chest. "Look John, I realize that I was a little hard on you the other day and old Benson mentioned that you had a strict deadline for an upcoming charity event you were stressing over. I had no idea that you were a magician. I still can't figure out how in the world you made all of those cigarettes disappear, and we saw you leave? That was amazing! I love and have been a fan of magic ever since I was a little kid! I'm sorry I didn't understand. I didn't know. You have quite a skill set son, I wish you would have mentioned that you needed time to prepare for your act. Anyway, I wrote everything that happened that day up as a minor incident. You're not terminated and you're free to come back to work whenever you're ready, John. You're a great worker, I appreciate all you do for us and would hate for this company to lose you. John, apologies… what do you say?" Mr. Hunnington looks him sincerely in the face.

"I say… yes, okay. Thankyou!" John shakes the bosses hand with great gratitude, sliding his check off the counter.

"No, thank you. Just leave the magic at home for now on. Or

tell me what you're planning!" John's boss winks and exits the office.

"Well aren't you the lucky one? Good for you. We all had our fingers crossed for you John." The secretary smiles and continues tending to her duties.

"Thanks." John leaves, and exits the building with a fresh cup of coffee.

"John! How's it going?" Old Mr. Benson leans against the main door, resting his aching back from mopping.

"Mr. B! Everything's great today! New day! Got my life back, job and a date!" John answers enthusiastically.

"Fantastic! How'd you do it?" Mr. Benson sticks the mop in the bucket, leaning its handle against the doorway.

"I went to the MAN, THE GREAT SOURCE, like you said. Well... like I thought you suggested to me the other day? Thanks Mr. B."

"Say no more, John. Between me and you, you must've heard what you needed to hear?" The old man smiles and wipes the sweat from his face. "You can never go wrong when you take the upper route, they say."

"It is a very wise saying, very true, very true." John nods, wearing a permanent smile.

"Care for a smoke?" Mr. Benson ask, placing his hand near his shirt pocket; a brief moment of silence breaks between them.

"Nah, I don't need that stuff anymore. I... don't smoke anymore, Benson. Guess... I gave it up." John couldn't believe the words coming from his lips. "I made someone a special promise."

"Good for you, John, because I don't smoke either." Mr Benson jokes, patting the flat pocket on is chest. "You know... I was thinking the other day, I mean... I know the cigarettes are bad for you, but... maybe you should slow down on the coffee too? I hear the latest research says caffeine is the latest drug. Bad for ya too now they say!" Old Benson looks down at John's coffee cup.

"You know what... listen, I've sacrificed, experienced loss,

I've walked through the fires of hell itself. I've been scared and humiliated to the worst degree, now... I'm going to tell you, Mr. Benson... there is nothing on earth that can take this simple cup of joy from me. Not even Satan himself can stop me from drinking coffee! I've been dragged through the mud and everything, I think I deserve this, old man!" John takes a large, hard sip from his warm cup as a stream of coffee runs from the seat of his pants, down his left leg. "Oh no... you! No!" John hollers and run off as hot coffee squirt and spray from various openings of his body. "Fire... ow, it's smoking hot! How is it even pouring from there!" John hurries up the street, holding the seat of his pants.

Mr. Benson, watching John rush frantically up the block, laughs to himself, tickled. Morphing into a faceless being of wisdom and divine light, he unnoticeably explode silently into a cluster of brilliant orbs. The form of spiritual energy ascends up the side of the building, vanishing in a scatter of particles and laughter.

The End

THE 12ᵀᴴ LANDING

A BLOODY MAN'S POEM

Just beyond old vine street cemetery,
buried beyond the shadows of unknowns deep,
a sleeping myth, an urban legend perhaps,
embarks upon a gruesome anniversary,
on old Mulberry street.

Once a year it was taught to every child and residence,
the unspeakable acts that happened upon that cold hill.
Unfortunate events, like the murders which had taken place
and rooted evil inside the buildings that slumber quiet and still.

One structure, a gray, purplish apartment complex,
which sat, singed from the outside in,
told of a forgotten time when an awful action
spawned from a terrible sin.

On that day, then, a man observes his neighborhood
filling with new faces and unwanted change.
Seeing parties and boozing with the mistresses of the night,
soured the mans spirits, his thoughts became deranged.

The man is shunned for his social indifference,
made a fool, outcast for the coming years.

Then one night, he is invited to a gathering but is tricked,
    embarrassed and tortured by his peers.

Some say it started from an argument,
    some respectfully argue it spun from a fight,
    yet all agree it must've been the devil
    that visited him on that night.

Inside an apartment raging of fire,
    Out of the darkness of death,
    limps a figure dragging a foot,
    with the eyes of evil itself.

Unbathed and unclothed;
    as it was to me told;
    a tall man stood, drenched of blood
    among the bodies the young and the old.

What could make a man commit such heinous atrocities?
    The headlines of the morning papers,
    ghastly with the horrible news,
    read, *found carved into a victims heart, a*
    single butcher knife was used.

Inflicting fatal injuries to his victims
    who bleed into a trail of fantastic red, colored pools,
He crept into the rooms of the judgmental and the teasing,
    stalking the nearby schools.

Yet, throughout the screams and senseless slaughter,
    and organs splattered across the buildings wall,
    no one could escape being thrown from the six floor,
    not one victim survived the fall.

And across the street where the second apartment lay,
It too faced the same fate.
The ambulance and fire department both responded to calls,
both reaching the crime scenes late.

No traces were ever left or found
of the suspicious person wielding the knife in hand;
only the bloody tales of the slain who witnessed
seeing the bloody man.

Unto this day, people say;
the screams of his victims can still be heard.
Do wrong by someone and someday you too may receive a visit,
silenced by your wrong choice of words.

But onward an on, into a new day and a dawn,
when you're alone and hear the screams along with the crying,
do not laugh, nor curse or point at a grave
or you too may be cursed with dying.

-thee end-

THE 13TH LANDING

HIGHWAY TO HECK

My bus driver's eyes seemed a little stranger than usual when I boarded the bus on Tuesday morning. I figured maybe she might have had a bad night's sleep or something, and didn't care to know about her private life or issues she might have been suffering. On our way back to school from embarking upon a routine fieldtrip to an opera, I sit on the Big Cheese with my friends, joking and socializing as usual. I glance at my friends Kelly, Tausha, Lakeisa and Christine, who sat with Claudia and Shonda; they were dance majors and also the smartest and most mature girls in my class. As a wade of paper flicks into Kelly's hair, half of the boys on the bus burst into a unified laughter. My friend Armand, who loves football and who s name was always called before mine, recites a rap song he wrote next to my pal, Tony and of course, Kwame, who was a spoiled yet cool, self-aware kid into art like me. In the midst of songs, jokes and conversation, I see a colorful container, next to a small red book, sitting in a wiry rack screwed into the middle of the buses dash board.

"Mrs. Cringe?" I stick my head up over my seat. "What's with the container?" I move a few seats up next to a friendly, tall guy named Jeremy who was quietly listening to his headset.

"Uh, it's special." The red headed woman quickly glances over at me, then quickly turn back to the road. "To tell you the truth, it's an urn."

"Who's in it?" I ask curiously, the entire front end of the bus grows quiet.

Popping a medium sized bubble of a bright pink colored gum, Mrs. Cringe gaze over into her rearview mirror at the traffic alongside the bus. "Boy, you sure got a lot of questions today. It's a loved one if you must know… my great grandfather. He was the only person in the world who cared about me. He was very special." She blinks several swift times as if her eyes were trying to water.

"What happened to him?" Hoping she would tell us something good, I cross my fingers next to Jeremy who now had his headset off and tuning in as well.

"Let's just say… it wasn't good." Her response kills half the buses attention, some of the students return to goofing off and being loud. "And this book, you see this book right here, it's just as special as he is." Mrs. Cringe's large hairy hand sways over the small book in the basket.

"What's it about?" I ask, doubting it was anything good at that point. I peer over at Jeremy who was returning to his heavy metal music.

"It's our history, a family treasure! It tells everything about my ancestors. I'm part Egyptian you know?" She winks and smiles.

"Thanks." I sigh, not believing anything she was telling me as we hit a bump. Watching the lid of the urn slightly lift open, I catch the tail end of something; a green mist escaping the jar being sucked into our bus drivers nostrils. "No, couldn't have." I think to myself, returning to my seat to sit with my class mates. Playing paper football with Clinton, a pint sized, dark skinned kid, learning the flute, I keep my eye on Mrs. Cringe from afar. I notice the large woman's right arm abnormally shaking. With her back to us, the bus driver watches oncoming traffic through the front window, steering steadily. The dark pupils of her lively, bright eyes, widen, turning her eyes entirely black underneath her eyelids.

When we ran the light on Central parkway and rounded the bin on two wheels, full throttle, I figured maybe she was just behind schedule, or perhaps her foot had slipped on the acceleration pedal. However, it wasn't until the school bus passed our high school, The School for the Creative and Performing Arts, that I knew something wasn't right. Maybe it was time for me to have a talk with our bus driver.

"Excuse me… excuse me, Mrs. Cringe?" Standing in the ale, I tap on her shoulder.

"Do you want to be eaten?" She hisses, guiding the bus onto the ramp of the interstate.

"This isn't the way to our school, you passed it! Where are you taking us?" I demanded answers.

"Kid…" She laughs, "Haven't cha figured it out yet? You are all going to die! Now sit down with the rest of the pigs!' The woman's face began to bubble, her arms and shoulders began to swell. Smacking me with her hand, Mrs. Cringe sends me flying backwards into the back of the bus. As my body hit the back doors, upon impact, the loud laughter and teasing on the bus break into a sudden silence.

Offended and embarrassed, bruised but not broken, I pick myself up, sucking my busted bottom lip. Thinking of my parents training, I feel myself slip into a teenage, disrespectful mode of conduct. "We're going to… what? Lady are you crazy?" I step to the side; preparing myself to counteract a terrorist attack. Mrs. Cringe slings her head to look at me. I observe her blank eyes change into a glowing, neon yellow, sending the hairs on my arms standing on ends. Suddenly, screams explode from every direction as the vehicle begins to swerve on and off the road. Swiftly crawling pass my friends, I climb into my seat next to Armand.

Looking at me with large bugged white eyes from behind a pair of black, thick framed glasses, Armand's extra-large football hands tremble inside his wide laps. "We're going to die, aren't we?" Armand, the same dark complexion as Clinton, short, solid in mass, with a passion for football, sat securely scrunched down inside his seat. Normally the most outspoken of the class, Armand sits frightened, tightening the seatbelt over his stomach. He glances at Mindy, a small, frail Caucasian girl, book smart with braces, turned backwards in her seat facing us.

"She's gone crazy hasn't she?" Mindy normally quite the quirky one, smiles deviously as the bus tilts, leaning everyone to one side. "She looks sick, I think she's infected."

"I bet she's drunk, and we're gonna crash in a second! Any last words?" Jason, a light skinned, chubby, curly haired, and mischievous student, in the heart of what could possibly be a potential kidnapping, gives us both a wet-Willy in the ears from behind. "What did you say to make her push you? I think we can take her?" Jason laughs as if it were all a game.

"Mrs. Cringe, this is not funny! You're going too fast, student's lives are in your hands!" We overhear Genevieve, a tall, skinny, and one of the best artist in our class, yelling. She stood up, holding onto the tops of the seats. Fearlessly, Genevieve faces the front of the bus. Licking her braces, her red face lightens; she prepares her next words. "Mrs. Cringe, right now, you're going through something. You can get through this and get better, but you need to stop the bus. I can help you, we're all here for you Mrs. Cringe, please…stop the bus." Genevieve feels the bus pick up more speed. "Mrs, Cringe! What's wrong with you, why aren't you listening? Stop the bus, you're going to fast, Mrs. Cringe!" Geneivieve heart pounds against her chest. She glances out the window at the rapidly passing trees and scenery outside flying by us.

"Look, smoke!" Drew, one of the shortest boys in our grade, points at the front of the vehicle. The bus vanishes into a thick mist of fog.

The heavy mist seeps in through the vents and openings inside the bus, gliding through the cracked, open windows. The fog blinds everyone including myself. I raise my arms, barely able to see my hands in front of my face. Listening for my friends, I hear them panic and crying out in fear all around me, then, all was completely quieted by a commanding voice.

"Everybody, just calm down!" Donte, an extremely large, muscular senior, well dressed, well mannered, and who also majored in band and dance, slowly steps towards the front of the moving bus. "Mrs. Cringe... Mrs. Cringe?" He calls out to the old woman, she doesn't respond. As the bus roll over large bumps, Donte utilizes the overhead railing to pull himself forward through the fog. "She's... she's gone?" His mouth drops open, speechless as he stare into the empty driver seat at the steering wheel. Rubbing the high faded box on his head, baffled, Donte sees the vehicle speed directly towards a cement divider. Crashing through a steel railing, the bus flips into a mad roll. The school bus collides into the ground, dispersing fire and smoke.

Sounds of killing and the horrific screams of my peers disturb a dream of my mother baking her most famous apple pie. From being knocked unconscious, I arose from a grave of burning metal, books, clothes and flesh. Shoving the body of a teenager off my legs, I flip it over, revealing the face of a classmate I was close to. Mortified, I crawl out the mangled wreck of the bus speedily. Pushing to my feet, I stand on side of the burning, smoking vehicle in confusion and frustration. Inside a flaming field of crashed school buses, miscellaneous cars and bodies, I watch my surviving friends scatter about, perhaps lost, in different directions. "What's happening... where are we?" I question the ALMIGHTY FATHER, hearing a faint sound of movement behind me. Turning, I see Mrs. Cringe. Standing near me, she grows several feet taller, sprouting long pointy horns from her wrinkled, pink forehead.

"Welcome to my hell. Now, you will pay for your sins!" Mrs. Cringe snarls a set of hideously uneven, jagged teeth.

Leaping from onside of the bus, I dive down into the wide

and long, steamy, ditch with others. Running through a field of automobiles, garbage and corpses, lost, I flee back into the fog. Stumbling over what appear to be graves and small headstones beneath my feet, I duck behind a tomb the size of a small cabin. Catching my breath, I gather my thoughts; a pair of large hands seize me from behind.

"Quincy! It's you! Thank GOD!" Jason leans his back against the tomb, thankful that he found someone else from the bus.

"Jason, where did everyone go? Why did they all split up?"

"Are you kidding me, didn't you see her, Mrs. Cringe? Where the heck you been at, man?" Jason wipes the sweat pouring from was face. "Where are we? It's hot down here! Wonder where all that fog come from?"

"I dunno but… I did see her. Well, I think I did… whatever that thing is she has changed into out there" I try to remember exactly what it was I saw.

"She came after you too? So you saw her then? This is crazy, why is she out to get us?" Jason trembles. "I saw her eat people, she ate our friend's right there in front of me! Anita, Antwan, Junisa…" He mutters.

Agreeing that it did us no good to stay where we were, we ran, under the moans of the dying and dead. Among the disturbing cries of students in the distance, we ran through that fog as far as our legs could carry us, until nothing but quiet was heard. Guessing everyone had been captured or killed, I thought of what the odds were that I would be the one left solely to survive with the obnoxiously irritating, class clown, Jason.

"I… I need to rest, dude, I can't go any further!" Jason collapse just ahead of a row of large crosses poking high from the ground. "We can't be in Ohio! Look at this place, where the heck are we? Where are the police?"

From the sight of blood and clots of fresh meat dripping down a nearby Stonehenge, I guessed Mrs. Cringe, or something else had gotten there before we did. "Uh, maybe we should rest somewhere else?" A body smashes into the ground, splashing Jason and I with body matter.

"You can run, but you will never escape!" Mrs. Cringe, perching upon the tallest cross standing crooked out the ground, stare down upon us. Busting out her uniform, she sheds her human skin, bringing forth a set of wing like appendages that jutted out from the back of a part human, reptile, and half beast looking creature. Roaring into the red colored sky, she spreads a wing span similar to that of a small plane. Diving down from the tall cross, a third arm with claws, jolts from her mouth at lightening speed. Nearly sending me into an early grave, I dodge the attack.

Feeling Jason's clammy hands pull me up, we flee through the nightmarish bog. Losing my footing, I trip and smash through coffins, plummeting down a sloping shaft of mud and gravel into a underground tunnel, feet beneath the dirt. Skidding, I slide and come to a stop. Peering inside the darkness, a loud yell brings me to my feet, alerted. Jason runs directly into me from out the shadows, sending me back down to the ground, sliding across a stone floor into a pile of decaying bones.

"Quincy? This is ridiculous! We're going to die in this place, man!" Jason shouts, scratched, bleeding and bruised.

Surprisingly, we discovered hanging torches, burning bright along the far walls of a connecting hall. A scatter of body parts cover the ground, seemingly frozen in an endless time. Limbs and the decaying faces of people seem to watch, and speak motionlessly as we pass, while the others slept secretly, half buried and exposed in their graves.

"I think we're underneath or... inside of some sort of old cemetery. We were just at school?" exclaims Jason.

"I know, right? Weird, looks like we're in some kind of ancient burial ground?" I respond as another head grows from Mrs. Cringe's shoulder, extending and lowering down into an opening in the ground, into the shaft exactly where we were.

"A soul for Hector, a soul for Hector! A soul for Hector!" The head chants as we flee off into the unknown darkness, hopefully leaving her far behind.

Tunnel after tunnel, level after level, we run, starting to become ill from the stench of rot. Occasionally hearing a scream or two, we chase the sounds into the empty and barren corners in hopes of saving at least one of our friends. Each time, finding ourselves back in the same foggy area in which we started, we begin to loose our sense of direction. Determined to go forward and to find our way, we try again and again, and dozens of times more, each time, coming to a dead end with still, nothing in sight to use for protection.

"Oh-crap, another dead end… again, what? We can't keep going on like this!" Jason squats down and rolls his shirt over his head. "Why is it so hot?"

"Look… up there, a door with one of those old locks on it. What's it doing here? I wonder what's in there, why didn't we see that before?" I point into the shadows at the remains of a small flight of eroded steps that led to a grim looking door. Ascending to the collapsed floor, I approach the door. Sliding a block of wood through two giant latches, I place the wooden board down softly by my left foot. Jason cracks the door open as I hesitantly peek inside. Adjusting to the blackness of the dark, I see a pair of running reptilian feet and legs carrying the upper body of Mrs. Cringe, heading directly for us in the doorway. "Shut the door, shut it! It's her!" I yell, slamming the door in Jason's face. "The latch, the lock!" I try to explain; Mrs. Cringe screams, trying desperately to push open the door with her mighty claws. Holding onto the handle with all of my reserved strength, Jason slides the wooden board between the doors latches, locking it back. Sighing, we ease carefully back down to the lower level of the tunnel from which we came.

"So much for getting out that way." I peer down at the mud and unknown muck covering my arms and clothes. "What are we going to do now?"

"We gotta get outta here, or she's going to kill us!" Jason blurts out, already in his third step towards doubling back.

"We need something to fight with, anything." I follow, becoming very concerned about our survival. "Grab a torch off the wall, we could use them as clubs, and to see our way." The ideal hit me as Jason catches on.

"How's about this metal pole?" Jason pulls on the handle of a lever protruding out of an opening near the base of a wall; a trap door opens, dropping us into the darkness below.

Falling down into a dark chamber, Jason lands on mound of bricks, old newspapers and dirt. In total darkness, I open my eyes to yet another round of pain, along with the burning sensation of dust inside my choking lungs. Feeling my way across the rough surface of a stone floor, the intensity of two large floating red lights, startle me. Quite angelic and mysterious, I wonder perhaps if we too had made it to heaven. I rub my hand across the sandy texture of the floor, finding the handle of my torch that still burned. "What are those?" I whisper, pointing the orbs. A loud shrill sirens loudly all around us. The room starts to rumble and quake, the floor shifts and splits. Mrs. Cringe rises from an explosion of rubble between me and Jason. Out of breathe, hope and energy, I finally release a scream in fright, as Genevieve does the same next to me.

"Quincy, it's you, you're still alive!" She finds me beside the torch.

"Genevieve?" I call out upon seeing her face under the torch light. She shoves me to the side as a large spiny tail slashes through the brick in front of us. "Wait… Jason? Jason!" I yell out as Genevieve shoves me into the burrow the monster just made.

"I'm good!" Jason's tiresome voice shouts out behind as we evade into the darkness of another underground cavern.

"Do you know where we are, have you seen a way out?" I ask. Genevieve swiftly hugs me tight. My hand touches a cut on her face, she flinches back.

Under the luminance of my torch, Genevieve clears the dirt from a wound on her leg with the inside of her shirt, and peers at me and Jason with pure desperation. "I... I found this book inside a room with the others. I took it before that thing could catch us. It's a little confusing, but there's some very interesting things in it... it's about her, Mrs. Cringe. She's mentioned in it several times by name. It says we're in some sort of ninth dimension, like an alternate realm or something? Maybe we could use something from it to defeat her. All I want to do is go back home. She killed everyone I was with. It was like, she was everywhere, able to move from place to place in a matter of minutes... like a phantom."

"Maybe she can teleport or walk through walls?" Jason steps behind us, trying his best to see ahead, under the flickering light of the torch.

"I don't know but one things for sure, she does possess magic." Genevieve, taller than me and Jason, hold on to one of my pipe cleaner arms, tightly.

Inside a deep maze of tunnels and unknown paths, we set out to find an exit from the hellish place. I begin to read pages from the book Genevieve acquired along the way, learning that the crazed bus driver was the granddaughter of Hector Cringe, a local businessmen and known worshipper of the black arts. With a love only for his granddaughter, it tells of how he makes a deal with a dark spirit to connect them together for all eternity. Murdered by his own relative and a group of unknown men in cold blood, before death, Hector vowed revenge on all the men who took part in the attack. He threatens upon the lives of their offspring's, and their offspring's alike, since he was violently stripped from his only child, his granddaughter. Upon his deathbed, I read: [He curses his own family, wanting them to join him forever in the afterlife.] For the favor, the book reads of how a demon exchanges power with him for his soul. It also tells of a relative from heaven, perhaps a guardian angel, who came down and hid a weapon to combat the evil inside a demons labyrinth. Unconvinced, I share the information with Jason, we compare mental notes about Mrs. Cringe with what Genevieve already knew. Knowing that if we were captured, we could be eaten, or worse, straight out killed, As we pick up the pace, loud bangs from the levels above began to knock dirt down from the ceilings above us.

"She's here!" Jason shouts out.

"She's found us!" I stand close to the last of my friends.

"You will never leave this place. Run… I have all eternity! Ha-ha-ha-ha!" The scary sound of Mrs. Cringe's demonic voice send chills up our spines.

"Uh-oh, I think she's broken through. She must be down here with us!" Jason panics as we scurry down the tunnels, through cobwebs, skeletal remains and a litter of organic matter.

"Be quiet, I don't see her." I whisper as we hid inside a blocked passageway. "She not attacking… why isn't she coming after us like the others?" I glance at Genevieve. She looks back at me as if I might have been on to something. It became blatantly obvious that we were being herded in a certain direction for a reason and was soon going to die. We agreed not to give up without putting up a fight; we decided an ambush was in order. Pulling as many torches from the wall as we could find, we guessed that a fire, and a stake to the heart should be able to do some sort of damage, according to the zombie and vampire movies we were raised upon. Jason and Genevieve, holding their noses and mouths, cleverly hid with the dead in the shadowy corners of the upcoming tunnel. Nearing an intersection of halls, I wait for the demon who seems to always find us, practicing batting the air with my torch. Quietly, I take my position; the sounds of crumbling dirt and a light rumble from the shifting of the earth, all become one continuous, soul numbing hum. Grow anxious with the rapidly growing fear, I know she's coming. Cold, hands trembling, I try to remember how I ended up there. "I was on a field trip." My lips utter my thoughts unconsciously out loud. I feel Jason and Genevieve's eyes stare at me blankly from down the dark corridor.

In a blink of an eye, in a whirlwind of blood orbs, Mrs. Cringe materializes around the corner from me. Slowly easing backwards into the shadows, I peep around the corner, gazing directly into her glowing cat like pupils. Spotted, the she runs my way. I club her deformed body with the torch, as Jason and Genevieve jump in. In breaking splintering wood and splashing fire, Mrs. Cringe's body ignites. Jason runs like a linebacker, jump kicking her flaming built torso backwards into the darkness. Genevieve quickly snatches hold to one of her long scaly necks. Then in a swift maneuver, I witness my innocent, nonviolent classmate and competitor in art, Genevieve, quickly put one of Mrs. Cringe's screeching and biting, fanged heads in a headlock. Even in the midst of darkness, my will to live couldn't let her stop me. I leap and catch hold to the howling twin head. As we pull the giant, chomping, fork tongued faces apart from each other, its burning body kicks and sways frantically. Jason finds a large, sharp edged stone, and slashes madly about, severing each head from the neck of their body. On fire, Mrs. Cringes body leaps from the floor, and runs down the tunnel wildly smacking into the walls; her two heads expel a foul wind and dying screams. Jason and I stomp the heads and neck into an unidentifiable pulp.

"We did it, yes!" Genevieve cheers as we high-five and hug each other.

"Got that witch!" Jason yells, "What now?" He pops his neck loudly as we stretch and bend our aching bodies.

"Finally!" Leaning over to touch my toes, my aching back pops. Under the dim lights of fire that still burned on the broken pieces of torch scattered across the floor, I notice a splatter of muscle and blood from the dead Mrs. Cringe, link and group together. Forming smaller, miniature versions of the slain bus driver, in disbelief, I squat down to get a closer look at what I think are tiny women, "Uh... guys, guys? I think you better come and..." the aura of a powerful presence overtakes me.

"Your time has come." Jason oddly blurts out. I spot the small clones of our bus driver running up his pants legs; Jason transforms into a large supernatural entity, Hector Cringe. Breaking through Jason's skin, a tall figure of an old man steps out. A massive spread of bat wings shoot out from his back as two spiraling antlers branch out above a thick forehead housing two angry red glowing eyes. "I will add your souls among the dead." Hector laughs; his voice rumbles through the tunnels collapsing ceilings and floors.

"Jason?" I stood helpless, unable to move. Feeling a tug, my body jerks in motion, my legs instantly paddle forward on their own accord. Pulling me by the hand, Genevieve releases her grip, Hector Cringe snatches her thin frame into the collapsing darkness. I hear her voice shout something from behind as I run. I stop, the toe of my shoe just touching the first step of a series of winding stairs. A gust of clean familiar wind blow down and across my body from the staircase, easily convincing me to peep up the unstable railing made solely of rodent bones. Seeing what appeared to be daylight at the very top of the stairwell, my heart, despite the dangers, knew it was the way home. With no time to morn my friends, I fearlessly climb the brittle staircase. My heavy, tired feet continuously break through the stairs with every other step to the top, but I still manage to make it to the entrance of light. "Another room?" I grumble to myself, unable to ignore a beautiful craved spear floating in mid-air, in the middle of the corridor ahead. "Wha... how did this get here? What does it mean?" I gaze, puzzled. The spear glimmered of reflective light, I approach it, entranced. Carefully, I examine it closely without touching, identifying the writing inscribed upon it as Egyptian. Its inscription, also matched the pictures and symbols I had seen in the Genevieve's book. Putting two and two together; bare handed, I take hold of the spear. The spirits of Donte and Mindy appear to me. Mindy frowns sadly, then scream without releasing a sound. Time for me, stopped the mere moment I saw them. Despite their beyond the grave messages I was ignoring, like a dream, I was happy seeing my friends again. Hector Cringe seizes me by the legs, snapping me back to reality. Tossing me back down into the staircase, I smash through the railing, managing to catch hold of a strand of rat bones with tfur and skin still attached. Disappearing above my head, Hector Cringe manifest beneath my dangling body. Pulling me downward, suddenly I am catapulted up through the remaining stairs and boney columns like a ragged doll. Hitting the ceiling of pure rock and hard earth, I feel gravity take its awesome hold on me. Catching a glimpse of Hector below my twisting body, tumbling, I try to catch hold to anything within reach. Finding nothing more than the spear still gripped tightly within my quivering clutches; I plummet downwards, down into the massive body of blackness. Preparing to swipe my flesh with his enormous hand of claws, Hector Cringe snarls in satisfactory. He swings, hopeless; I pierce his dark center with the spear, crashing through the lower levels of stairs.

In a shower of tiny bones and dust, wedged between the wall and Hectors enormous horns, I witness his large body fold below me in a loud roar of howling souls, dissipating into tiny orbs of energy. Tumbling through the spectacle of lights, I fall below to a hard stone floor. Stunned that I was still alive, I sit up and feel around with my hands, realizing that I was actually resting on an enormous old tomb. Sliding down its side to my feet, I dust off and lower myself even more carefully down to the next roof of a small stone cottage looking structure still fused to the side of the tomb. With crosses on all sides of the building, I eye another large cross protruding from its center. Yet, for some reason, I felt safe. Posting on the edge of the structure, I pondered on what to do next. A sudden strong force shoves me off; I am sucked into the closed door below. Breaking through a thick layer of stone and wood, I hurtle towards what could only be describe as an enormous mouth. A long salivating, freckled tongue swept the empty space in front of me. Spinning out of control, I grab and hang on to its slimy surface for dear life. Helplessly, I dangle across an giant open throat that tries to swallow me whole. I can see Genevieve's red book inconveniently sitting in back of the tongue, hung up on dead bodies and limbs. "How'd it get here?" I think to myself with no time to answer. Diving onto a large tooth, I squeeze between bone, stretch and grab hold of the book. Securing my footing, I quickly fumble the book open. Its pages blow in the mighty current of the circulating wind. The ghost of the Mrs. Cringe whom I remembered, flies out the book and hovers down to me.

"You must stop my grandfather. Stop him from gaining more power. He's not defeated." She spoke in a glowing colorless figure.

"Stop him? But I killed him? Wait... how? I already speared him."

"He may have taken our bodies, but as a spirit, some of us are free. The more souls he collects, the more powerful he will become. Soon, everyone alive will all be in jeopardy. The more he consumes, the sooner he can open the gates of hell and free the demons even more sinister." Mrs. Cringe explains.

"But... how? What can I do?" I clung for dear life as the tongue begins to retract into the now chewing mouth.

"You can defeat him. Connect the path of the dead to the path of the living. From there, I will assist you. Force him out into the real world and he will be powerless. Now go!" The middle aged woman launches forward as if she was going to attack; I lose grip of the giant tooth, vacuumed into the belly of the unknown creature. Whirling within its intestines, I journey to a remote realm inside its body. Floating inside a breathable atmosphere of internal tissue, muscle, veins and electrical surging nerve endings; I land like a feather upon an old brick road next to Hector Cringes slain body. Side stepping around him, I think about Mrs. Cringe's words. I glance over at the sight of the real world that I call home sitting on the other side of a portal just ahead. Stepping down on a protruding brick sticking up from the ground, it presses down into a fitting slot in the street like a puzzle piece. The portal to my world fades behind a thick mist of smoke as the supernatural body of Hector Cringe rises from his dead corpse. Dropping another unfortunate student from his mouth. Charging at me, a great force launches me into the air, appearing over me, Hector smacks me down to the bricked road just a few feet away from the portal home. Lifting my head to face my death, I see Mrs. Cringe smiling just behind Hectors shoulder.

"You cannot defeat me. You shall not pass!" Hector swats at me again. Slicing through my clothes, I am slung to the opposite side of where I was. Approaching to finish me off, our surroundings transform into a familiar place. The smell of fresh flowers hit me as the brightness of the Sun blur my vision. I make out the tall, vividly green grass and tar around me. Realizing that I was on the interstate, I dodge a heavy rush of traffic that appear out of nowhere. Turning my head, I see the eyes of Hector Cringe. Powerless in the real world, Hector screams in rage as a Semi-truck strikes him. Banging his soft, fleshy body like a pinball, against the closet passing vehicle, the truck knocks Hector into going and oncoming traffic. As he is torn and splattered across the road, I watch the freeway jam and come to a complete stop over the sight. Sad over the loss of my friends, I smile, relieved that it was all over. I had successfully survived the trip down the highway to hell. Missing the faces of my friends, I hold out my thumb over the open road to hitch a lift home. Gazing forward, slowly I step down the highway alone, under dozens of flying demons fleeing from hundreds of portals opening in the sky. Like bats flying in waves of drones below the clouds, in a loud screeching, howling chorus, the winged creatures descend from the sky upon the city.

The end`

THE 14TH LANDING

AWAKENED

Some say you can hear the heart of a storm before it comes. Its heart, beating like speaking Indian drums during the coming of water spirits, as the rain drizzle against my building. It is also said that if you listen hard enough, you can hear your soul speaking to you. I listen, I hear nothing. I even speak to my body, but still, it still refuses to respond as it use too. I'm sick, and cannot pin point what this illness is I feel, so... I decide to confide my troubles in the ears of a trusting open minded listener. I indeed needed someone to talk to.

My dark, red stained hands suggest I either helped someone or a made them a victim. The thirstiness in my eyes hold no discrimination as the sweat pour from my pores, drenching clothes and sling from my limp body I drag across the floor. (Hell has no bounds) I remember someone once telling me. My eyes, twitchy, hands, painfully weak, and my legs, heavy and cold. Memories of a woman, my girlfriend Sade, fade away as I lose control of my thoughts. I drop hold of my friend who was a corpse, stepping over a fresh dead body, my bloody feet dragging when I walk. "What's happening to me?" My joints stiffen, bones aching and cracking loudly. A bone breaks through the skin when I bend my knee. I find a piece of a glass mirror in my chest, the beauty of its shimmer takes away from the bright blood I see underneath my hoody. The way the color crawled down my clothes, was just like how the dark droplets of water ran down and saturated the stone bricks of my apartment when it rains.

It appeared I still remembered where I lived for the past, previous years; the complex stood quiet inside a light steamy fog. "Why was I outside?" I couldn't figure it out, all I knew is that I had to lay down fast. Usually upon arriving close to house, the poodle of Judy Englemen, who lived on the first floor, would bark in the front window until she calmed it. But tonight it was nowhere in sight. While my spine crackled to the melody of shifting out of place bones in my back, I hobble, slightly delusional and hurting everywhere, towards the apartment. Clumsily tripping over the side bushes, I tumble to the ground, hearing a snapping sound. On my back, I attempt to move my neck first; an unbelievable sensation of pain travel down my spine and across my shoulders. Moving my legs and right arm, I realize that I wasn't moving them at all. I only thought they were moving in my imagination. Wet, extremely cold and severely cramping, I go into shock, paralyzed, I lay there motionless in the rain.

Water gather and stream down upon my tilted head and face. I make out a desperate stray cat scrounging for food. Unable to move, I watch it decide if it should explore my facial area. Appreciating what I think are my last minutes of peaceful life, I smile at the feline. As the cat comes extremely close, I instinctively snatch its head off instantly with my right hand and mouth. Uncontrollably devouring its small plump body, I indulge in the sweetness of its blood and the tenderness of succulent muscles. Gorging, I fall back slightly fulfilled, temporarily rejuvenated and pain free. Suffocating in pouring blood and organs, I go for the small hind legs I left. Thinking about the gruesome act I'm committing, I try to gain control of my ravenous appetite. Dropping the empty carcass onto the pavement, disgusted, I realize what I have done and blackout.

Total darkness and tranquility is all I see and feel. Then suddenly a chill returns to my body to the touch of extreme cold.

Sparkles of light glitter in my eyes as I awaken underneath the stars. In the backyard of my mother's old house, I lay in the grass awaiting my brother to come out. As a loud horn of a truck sound from everywhere, I snap out of the daydream. I catch a glimpse of a blue, full sized truck driving full speed in my direction. Sitting up, slow and stiff, limbs as heavy as clay, I stand; the approaching truck, coming nonstop, forces me to dive out of its way. The vehicle crashes into a nearby building across the street. Again I shove myself up from the ground, staggering to the front door of my apartment complex. Hearing an odd set of shifty footsteps, I turn to a familiar face behind me. Glancing over my shoulder I see my neighbor from down my street. It was Mr. Davis, split from the forehead to his chin. While he stood staring at me as if trying to figure me out, I squat down and pick up a nice size stick. "Mr. Davis… you okay? Looks like you need a doctor? I do too. What's… what's happening to us?" I ask, looking into his hungry, confused, dark raccoon eyes. Stumbling out of the now overturned truck behind me, inched another injured soul. Spotting me, he holds out his hand to speak, but before any word could be said, a passing teenage girl attacks him. As the injured man fight her off, I observe Mr. Davis eagerly run to assist him. I was too drained to help. "There you go, be careful Mr. Davis." I mumble. Barely able to keep my balance, I fall forward, smashing through the thick glass doors like a rock.

"What a day." Suddenly aching tremendously all over, I sigh, finding myself stepping lead footed to the elevator. "My body, why does it hurt so much?" Too weak to take the stairs, I lean against the wall, pressing the button to summon the elevator. As my hands sweat and body shiver in coldness in the middle of summer, a buzzer rings from over me as the doors open up. Upon entering, I notice a little boy and a small little girl inside. Breaking into a feverish sweat, I lean upright to keep my head up. With one eye open, I could see that the little girl of around the age of six, was crying, and didn't look so well. "What's wrong with her?"

The doors close. I press the button to my floor, beginning to see various blotches of colors around the confined space. "What's the matter kid... cat got your tongue? No need to be scared, I wouldn't hurt a fly." I attempted to befriend them as their mouths just hung open at either the fact I looked like some sort of wasted junky, or they were staring at me because of the large bone protruding from my leg. My body, numb in places I had forgotten, took the attention off the leg and the crunching sounds it made every time I moved. "How'd it get broken?" I couldn't remember. Waking up in the middle of the street suggested to me, that I might have been struck by a car or ran over by a Trolley or something. The bell sounds as the elevator stops on the third floor. The little girl watches me from the corner of her eyes as she and the little boy slowly ease out.

So tired, weak, my mind drifts, eyes close, I hear the sounds of steel door close gently. I lean against the wall for support. Listening to my loud gurgling heart, I feel its rhythmic pattern slow down drastically; scaring me. The door reopens. Pushing off the carpeted wall, I head for my apartment. My neighbor's small, round dog dash between my legs. Before I could catch it, the canine slams into the elevator door, lodging its head, between the door and its frame just before it closes. Kicking and yelping, the pooch rises to the ceiling, its body drops loosely to the floor. The elevator continues on its way as the body of the pet quivers in a pool of its own blood.

It appeared that everything seemed to be quite normal except for anything else that crossed my path. My hallway maintained its own normality, except for some of the televisions that were turned up unusually loud inside the other apartments on the floor. Hearing radio broadcast and special news bulletins, oddly enough, they were all discussing the same topic, the latest flu vaccine. Some sets were on real sounding entertainment shows, but due to my own issues, I had no interest in investigating the noises. I was sick and head was spinning, but still, I managed to find my way to the door. My door, locked, exactly how I left it, except it wasn't completely closed. A window left open on the inside viewed flakes of chipped wood and sawdust along its frame indicating a force of entry. Broken glass crackle beneath my feet as I stumble into the hallway. "Charlie?" I call out, entering the living room. My "27" inch television that normally sat on a black stand inside of my bedroom, as if flung by a muscle bound man, sat inside a large hole in the middle of one of my walls. The floor model television inside my living room lay on its back in the middle of the floor with two kitchen chairs, broken and crammed through its center. My heart began to beat once every thirty seconds, I start to lose conscious in and out around the room. Charlie, my cat, stretches out on my couch, silently foaming at the mouth, eyes, bloodshot, rolled to the back of his head. Backing away from the sick, beloved animal, I couldn't even cry as Charlie gurgles his last meow, dying quietly on the cushion of my couch. Slipping on a stainless steel spoon, I glance at the trail of silverware scattered about the floor leading into the kitchen. Apparently a struggle had taken place and from the look of the blood seen under my overturned fridge, someone was definitely trying to stop someone else. A leg was missing from the dining room table as it sat overturned, resting upon two broken chairs. A mixture of bloody and clean cookware stabbed into the wall next to my picture, as more holes led to the oven, which wore a large dent in its door that was ripped from its hinges. Electricity sparked and flickered inside the running microwave; I turn its power off and gaze through its busted window at a spoon which sat inside a bowl of liquid I could not distinguish. A thick trail of red stretch from the kitchen counter into the sink, like a horror scene. Moving near the dish rack, I notice two twitching fingers inside the garbage disposal. As blood from my head drip into the sink, a shredded stub of a hand tries to leap at my face. Hollering, I shove it inside the drain and turn on the disposal and hot water.

The sink clink and clangs, sputtering blood over me and onto the ceiling.

The whole day so far seemed like a dream, it was like I had been drifting through a time warp. I couldn't believe the weird things were happening all over. My apartment looked like a murder mystery, and I didn't know who's hand it was inside my sink. A finger falls off and lands by my foot as a solid gold ring on its knuckle catches my attention. Bending over to look, blood and small pieces of my organs pour from my mouth onto the floor. I fumble through the vomit to retrieve the ring. It was something about the ring that drove me, attracted me, it was special, but I was clueless to why. A deep watery growl rumbles .inside me, I turn as Charlie my black and grey, long haired cat, oddly hisses. Snatching up the finger into its mouth, he runs off. I catch him by the scruff of his neck and attempt to retrieve the finger from its mouth. Charlie claws my face, the ring tumbles and bounces against the floor. Staggering back, I watch the cat swallow the finger whole and flee into the shadows under my furniture. "Dumb cat!" I wave him off and turn to the bathroom to clean up and take some medicine. "A few bottles of aspirins should put me out for a few hours, or until I find a doctor. Hell, I ain't trying to die in an ambulance or hospital, my bed is fine. I just want to sleep and forget about everything." I thought to myself, entering the bathroom. Inside the darkness, I stood over the toilet to urinate. Lifting up the toilet lid and then seat, I turn the lights on over the tank as a woman's head glances back from under the depths of the bowel. Her mouth open and close, her teeth chattered inside bloody water. It was my neighbor, who was the owner of the dog that lost its head in the elevator. Flushing the toilet, I slam the porcelain lid down hard, breaking it in half. A light tapping caused me to turn. The headless body of the woman attempts to remove itself from my shower, still trapped behind the closed glass doors. Turning the water on somehow, it slips to the red covered floor, splattering blood across the door. Suddenly receiving flashes of letting the woman in, I remember her attacking me, biting a chunk out of my arm. Lifting my sweatshirt sleeve, I reveal sets of teeth marks and a large plug shaped like a mouth, missing from my left arm. "What's happening?" I still couldn't put it together. "Did the woman pass me a disease?" I began to worry, touching the blade of the meat clever that was used to cut off her head. "I ate a cat." I slowly rewound my memory. "She bit me and her body came after me. It threw me out... of ... the window? She bit me." I then remember the details of my most recent misfortunes. "What's going on? What am I then?" I question and tune into the licking sounds coming from behind me. Crouching down, I spot Charlie licking from a puddle of blood on the floor. As his beady eyes met mine, he hisses and meows threateningly. I could see a patch of skin and fur missing from his hide. From the deranged feline, my eyes pan to my neighbors head floating in the overflowing toilet. "Charlie!" I politely call to my cat as his tail puffs out aggressively as it blocks the bathroom entrance with its body. Spitting up bodily fluids just like me, Charlie shivers and twitch erratically. Sniffing the wind between us cautiously, slowly the feline approaches me. Reaching down to my loyal companion, he leaps into my arms and licks my face just like he always does. Somewhat relieved by his presence, I kiss Charlie on the top of his head. Charlie growls, claws out one of my eyes and sinks the sharp fangs of his teeth, deep into my face. Receiving a new sensation of pain, I scream, slinging the feline into the next room. Charlie takes a piece of my top lip with him. Going for the pistol hidden beneath my bathroom cabinet, angrily, I load it with ammo and cock it. Covering my mouth with one hand, I lurch into the living room to put down my beloved pet.

Charlie, unable to get enough of my taste, bite into the juiciness of my injured leg as I step over the big screen television on the floor. I blow his small body into kingdom come, leaving a new hole burrowed through my floor. Sensing my blood as well, was my neighbor's head in the toilet, her body, breaks free from the tub and comes after me. Oh how I began to hate the dead, I felt the dislike fill inside me as I fire into the heart and body of the woman multiple times. Opening a mouth where her head should be, the half-naked body charges at me like a four legged beast. The torsos arm knocks me across the room, breaking my jaw and fracturing my face. Still, rising to my feet, I stand as it charges me again. Off balanced, I take hold of the arm of the woman whom I desired two years ago. Swinging in a circular dance of undiscovered and unfound love, I fling her body out my closed window.

"So this is what becomes of me?" It dawned on me what was going on; I walk over and hike one leg onto the window ledge. My tired, watery eyes gazes over of my chaotic town. Bodies descend passed my window to the ground as I overlook the burning buildings throughout the city. I return to the bathroom medicine cabinets for more bullets. Blood ridden water overflows from the toilet, my neighbors floating and bobbing head tries to feed on the same blood it was drowning in, inside the bowl. Loading my gun, I looked at myself in the mirror for the last time. Gazing over at each other, I and the head, her eyes meeting mine from between a mess of floating tangled hair. Having no limbs, she stretches her tongue out the water to taste my air, the bowl explodes from one shot of my gun. Going into my room, I open up my window as wide as I could, blasting down two strange people climbing up my building. Accepting the world's fate as my own, I hold the gun up between my eyes. Listening for a moment, my heartbeat stops, I know it has begun. I fire one shot directly into my head. "Heaven must be dark." Are my last thoughts, as a tiny ball of light appears ahead. Growing bigger and bigger, getting closer, I accept the light as my end. Warmness overcomes my body, followed by that same familiar freezing cold I always felt. From the darkness, I awaken in front of a mirror. With an eye still intact but hanging out from my head; I see my thin body viciously tackle a screaming person to the floor.

They scream, "Zombie!" as I uncontrollably eat at their neck.

{"They want us dead."} I overhear a news broadcaster on a busted radio during his mention of the recall of millions of vaccines. As the broadcaster warn the public of a new dangerous outbreak from the recent flu vaccinations, I witness myself break down someone's front door, and carry them away into the unknown darkness of the night.

The End

THE 15TH LANDING

ROAMERS

A ballroom dance and a gentle touch was complimented with a candle lit dinner, a smoke and a stroll. From afar, the main entrance, illuminated with bright bulbs, reminded her of the beauty of the brightly lit stars in the night sky. In an alleyway, as he leans in for a kiss which was soon to be the last contact of their lips touching, sounds of thunder and the brilliance of lights cast upon them multiple times. He falls into her arms, gaze into her eyes; both lives now separated. Clutching his chest, he struggles to speak important last words from his voiceless mouth. She looks down at his black tie and white suit stained of speckles of wine. Entranced in the brown eyes she thought she would spend the rest of her life gazing into, it pains her to even think of ever letting him go. Catching a glimpse of a man pillaging the pockets of her love while she lay there helplessly with him, she sees a blurred dark figure also standing over them. Before she could even react to fight off the robber, the tall figure behind them raises his hand. Everything flashes white again under the sounds of a large cannon. Holes rip into her dress. Her grip loosens from around her husband's head, he slips from her hands and finger tips; she falls back, alone and numb.

"Get up." She twitches and moves to the sound of a tiny voice. "Why don't you just get up?"

"I once knew the FATHER. I once... knew HIM." A deep, dark and demonic voice jolts her closed eyelids open.

The street, even more surreal, different and seemingly unrecognizable at first, darkened as she lay on her back, facing the night sky. Fighting to breathe, she watches her husband gurgle a raspy breathe of wind next to her bleeding body. Heart weakening, legs trembling, she finds the strength to turn her head.

"If you stay here, you'll forget your purpose." A little girl hid in the shadows behind a garbage can in front of an old building, underneath a window. "Stay there, and you'll face your fate."

Wondering why she couldn't really move, the woman touches her husband's hand, noticing a man with a gun, hop into a car. Glimpsing at the dented and bent plates on the vehicle, she watches the car pull off and drive up the block. As the dark figure, faceless, retreats into a vacant building just up the street near where the car turned, her bloodied, revengeful hand reaches for them, her head falls against the warm tar surface. Laying in silence, thinking about her life, her love, and her loses, a small light gleams brilliantly from out of thin air. A sense of love and peacefulness suddenly engulfs her, making her feel as if she was in the warm presence of her late passing mother. Turning back for one last glance at her husband, a single tear trickles down her cheek. Her mouth quivers to speak as she witness the soul of her husband raise into a firm beam of light and energy that streamed from the open heavens. To her, it only could have been the works of GOD who came to get her husband; she lifts a hand to the transparent winged figures that fluttered about them. One angel, a flawless and perfectly built handsome young man, looks down at her in pity. Another, a beautifully glowing entity, a woman with curly locks, smiles down at her as she sobs fearfully, unprepared to be raptured into the afterlife. Her husband's lifts his head, he sees her, saddened, he breaks a smile as the spirits vanish into the light with him in a burst of dark, screeching and shrilling sounds. Absorbing the magnitude of what she just experienced, the woman mentally tries to comprehend what was happening to her, feeling as though she was left. Suddenly, the atmosphere slightly lightens, she was back in the alleyway next to her husband's body.

"Go?" A cloud of darkness fell over the woman's head. Slowly, she lifts up. As people gather around her and her husband's body, she overhears someone calling an ambulance.

"You can see their souls, but they can't see yours." The little girl dressed in an old German school dress whispers to her.

Ignoring the voices, memories of her husband play over again in the woman's mind. Flashes of her husband's death and the building in which the killer fled, stabs at her heart and conscience. Knowing that the authorities would not be much help, she decides to go after him. In no pain, neither warm nor cold, she picks herself up from the ground. Confused and lost in emotions, she runs in the direction of the attackers escape route. Unsure of everything, she flees the scene with a sense of near dying, never once checking her wounds. Not looking back, she runs, leaving her and her husband's body behind. In half stride, she spots a bent license plate in the middle of the road. Memorizing the number, the sounds of fire trucks and police sirens fill the background of people. Mentally drifting and detached from the life changing event that just occurred, the woman knew leaving the scene of a murder was a crime within itself, but she had to find the murderer. Although she wasn't guilty, she knew that eventually she would have to answer for her actions, but she didn't care, someone took her love. Where she was going, she didn't know for sure, what she would encounter, didn't matter to her heart. All she knew for certain was that she wanted to know who took her husband from her and why? Knowing she had no place chasing any man, nor a killer for that fact, the burning desire to bring them to justice she felt inside, ate at her sense of reasoning and logic, bravely she ran under the street light.

"She will forget." A old woman's shaky voice mumbles into the air.

"What's your decision?" The little girl huddles behind a

parked car near the woman. Her silhouette crawls underneath the automobile as the woman now finds herself stumped, with nowhere to go. "Welcome to the valley of death, I knew you would stay." The little girl laughs as the street lights go out around the woman and everything fades to black.

Upon the sidewalk, the woman eyes the weird change to her surroundings, everything was extra spooky and weary looking. "Who's talking? Where are you?" her voice echoes into infinity. "What's happening to me?" She looks up at the swirling purple sky.

"I used to know things, but now, I don't remember much." The little girl responds from inside the car. "You better hide now, we aren't the only ones out here."

"What... little girl..." Discombobulated, the woman stares at the row of nearby housing she thought the mysterious man fled into. "Which way did he go? Where is that bastard?"

"If I were you, I'd stay away from the light." An old woman dressed in rags with an old green knitted hat, hobbles by and disappears in the entranceway of the large, abandoned brick building in front of her.

"Wait, who are you? What... she's gone?" The woman stares at the building puzzled. "What's happening?"

"They're coming." The woman see's the little girls tiny eyed oval face vanish inside the car, she hears loud banging sounds coming from the shadows and buildings around her.

"What are you doing in that car with the windows up? Did someone lock you in there?" The woman steps to the transparent window of the automobile. "Little girl? Hey, that's really dan... no way... gone." She steps away frightened. Two young men walk by joking with one another; the woman tries to ask them for help. "Hey, excuse me? Please help me. My husband..." She steps in front of them; they pass through her body unfazed. "Oh my-gosh, I'm seeing ghost and... spirits? No!" Chills shoot up her spine, she rubs her arms for comfort and gathers herself together. The loud sounds, now followed by weary screams, intensify. "Help,

help me!" She yells at strangers socializing outside, up and down the street as they try to figure out why police cars kept driving by. No one hears her or even budges to acknowledge her cry. Then, a very loud and heavy crash rumbles the street in every direction, cracking the ground and splitting the walls of buildings. Peering at the people outside still standing calmly in place, she feels the strong sensation of being watched. The flapping of large wings sound in her direction from the darkness beyond the street. Then, a variety of animalistic noises and the sound of a large object like a bull dozer, hitting the apartment across the street, sends her shuttering in front of the buildings. Pushing off a street sign, the woman hurries to the entrance of the abandoned building where the old woman fled, dozens of spirits squeeze through the doorway with her. Falling onto a floor of dead bodies, she quickly stands, finding herself in an old lobby. Orbs of lights swiftly vanish into the shadows of the ceilings and torn wallpapered walls.

"They're coming." A eerie voice whispers in the wake of several slamming doors.

Stepping over faces of a timeless moments perhaps forgotten and buried, the woman step and leap over the stiff limbs, frozen in place as if they were glued to the misty floor. Unable to avoid most of them, bones crack and snap like twigs below her, as she makes her way down a hall of flickering lights. Wondering how she couldn't see the ceiling lights from the outside of the building, she turns into a dark walkway. Something moves along the floor as she passes, she spins around to see what it was; a pair of legs bend in the darkness.

A homeless looking man in tattered clothing, reeking of liquor, inches out the entranceway. Missing three fingers, holding a dirty rag over his mouth, he points the hand with the two remaining fingers directly in her face. "It is you, I can see you. You're one of them Roamer's aren't cha?" He mumbles in a muffled sound. The sight of his permanently sealed eyes come into focus under the light; "You can see and hear me as well too can't cha? HE will find you. You can't prolong it. You will not escape judgement. I can see you." He reaches for her. "You shall not pass the fire! I'm not crazy, I see you, abomination!" the rag lowers, revealing an infected ridden mouth missing sections of the lower jaw bone.

Horrified, the woman draws back in a scream. Dashing away, a small set of hands seizes her face, yanking her through the wall by the head. In a cool tingling chill of emotions and sounds of past events and times captured within the very fiber of brick within the wall, she connects with it, experiencing the lives of different families and people. She materializes out the wallpaper on the other side. "Wha… what's going on? How did I…" She holds up her hands covered in her own blood. "What is this?" She peers down at the holes in her dress.

"You're dead. Stay with me." The old woman in the knitted hat and sweater appear behind her with rats trampling down out her of long stringy white hair, down her arms. As the rodents disappeared beneath the hags clothing and sleeves, pigeons cooed from her shoulders and from half dead looking birds grouped at her feet.

Before the woman could scream again, a slight force pulls her through the low ceiling. Inside what used to be the bedroom of an efficiency apartment, the woman is gently held against the floor with the little girls hand pressed against her mouth.

"Hush, they'll hear you." The little girl dressed in a short dark blue dress with white socks pulled up to her knees, eases off of her. A slender slit in the middle of her throat overspills of black blood; she crawls towards the furthest wall. "Pay the old woman no mind, some of the lost ones are attracted to you."

"No, how? I'm… I'm… d, d, d,…dea…" Going into shock, crawling away slowly on her back in the opposite direction of the small child, floored by what she was seeing, the woman escapes through a cracked open door. "This can't be real." Poking her head into a long hall, an immense light fills one end of the hallway. A sense of love and peace envelopes her again, she smells roses and a hint of light incense.

As the intensity of the growing brightness began to bend the hallway walls outward around it, a man dashes out of a room near it. A glowing winged figure manifest from the light in front of the man. "I'm ready!" Are the last words the man utters as the glowing deity pins him to the wall by the neck. The woman catches a glimpse of the winged figures beautifully wickedly sneering face. She is snatched back into the room, the door slamming shut behind her.

"You shouldn't get too close to the light. They will find you and eat you." The old woman whispers into her ear, covering her mouth with a filthy hand; the man in the hall howls in a scrutiny of pain. "Now quiet, they're coming!"

Huge splits streak and open along the walls of the bedroom as the woman watch the ball of light pass their position in the hallway, underneath the crack at the bottom of the door. Upon its departure down the hall, the woman hears sounds of laughter and scratching as two sets of eyes peer into the room just before the cracks reseal along the wall. The beams of light vanish and space quiets as the woman observes the room magically heal itself. "I'm... I'm dead?" The woman looks at the child and old woman dumbfounded. She then remembers a gun being drawn at her, next to her husband; she touches the bloody bullet wounds along her body. "We were murdered?" She tries to remember what had brought her inside the building in the first place. Flashes of a faceless person beside the murderer in her mind verified that she had died and reminded her of what she came to do. "I'm dead, unbelievable! How the hell are we still living? I mean... I'm still right here, I'm still me? Those men walked right through me, or I... passed through... no. I'm me... and you're... you... dead too?" She thinks of her husband being carried off by winged people, then remembers suffocating, taking her last breathe.

"Who are you and what the heck were those things in the hall?" She whispers rubbing her neck.

"They are the enlightened ones, do not go to them if you want to live. Now shush. Hide, they're here." The little girl quickly began to float around the room in search for a hiding place.

"Come... stay with me." The old lady tugs on the woman's arm, she pulls away disgusted. The old woman dematerializes into the carpet on the floor.

"I thought they passed, are they coming back? What are we hiding from, more enlightened ones?" The woman hears a heavy pounding against the building. "What is that?"

"It's a sign they have arrived." The little girl freezes in place.

"Who... more enlightened ones?"

"No, them..." The little girl points to a single busted window in the far wall. "The fallen." She disappears behind the woman as she walks up to the window sill.

"What on earth are those?" The woman see's strange silhouettes of creatures climbing on the rooftops of buildings and walking along the streets outside. "Demons?" She utters as her heart drops. "Are those de... little girl?" The woman steps away from the window, glancing around the quiet emptiness of the room. Sweeping her hand across an old tilting dresser, small puffs of collecting dust raise under the passing wind created by her fingers. Stepping around a dusty wood framed bed, a ticking noise from the closet startles her. Curious as to rather or not it was the little girl, she walks over and pull on its brass knob, feeling resistance, it slams close with great force. Deciding to leave it alone, she tread slowly into the connecting living room hoping not to be found by a demon. Keeping low, she notices there were no windows in the room. Oddly, as if her mind was playing tricks, she makes out two shadows squatted down in the corners; they move and shift in the darkness as she draws closer.

"What are you doing here? They're going to find us because of you!" The shadow on the left, crinkled and bent, harps out at her.

"We were here first, get out!" The shadow on the right, smaller, curvier, in the shape of someone wearing a brim hat, folds and arches a set of mean glowing eyes. "You don't belong here. This is our spot!" The shadow expands covering half the room with pitch blackness.

The woman is shoved, then pushed through the wall beside her. Unable to make heads or tails of what was up or down, she crashes into the tiled floor, slamming her head into the next wall. Standing up, she wondered how she collided into the wall when she just fell through one. Inside a doorway, she looks around scared and frightened inside another hall. A few feet away from a demon tormenting a poor wandering soul.

Spiny along its head and body, legs bent opposite of humans, the scaly faced, blue tinted creature curls a smile of sharp jagged teeth in front of the helpless soul. "How long did you think you could hide, all eternity? Your time on earth is spent, you pathetic monkey worm!" Legs bent back like the hind legs of an insect, the demon slams the man to the floor and drags him down the hall by the ankles. The light flickers and walls began to split and crack open with beams of light ahead of them. The demon draws back in fear. "Looks like we have other plans for you. Go meet your worthless maker."

"No!" The man screams as the demon tosses him into the surging ball of light. Sensing another presence, the demon skims the area for hidden spirits. Seeing nothing, the creature is repelled from the pure radiance of the enlightened ones. Spotting the woman in the shadows of the hall, the light streaming from the cracks along the wall began to burn the demons rough skin. Roaring at the woman, displeased, the demon falls back as the man screams in torment. Sneakily, the creature evades the light and eases into the open door of another apartment, and out the nearest window in a ill hardy burst of laughter.

The hall fills with an intensity of brightness, a door could be heard opening in the same direction. Quickly the woman scoots backwards into a stairwell and runs up the steps. Upon reaching the next level, she peers over the banister and eyes the little girl hovering at the top of the staircase. "Lil girl!" The woman blurts out in a low voice, not wanting to get noticed by any unwanted spirits. "No!" The child vanishes from sight, the woman heads up the next flight of stairs after her. Making it to the top level, she enters a door to the floor. Dark, damp, and condemned to all living trespassers to the highest degree, the floor sat caving in, with sections of its ceiling missing. Inside a long dark hall of doors, some doors missing, the woman notice some portions of the wall dripping of what looked like blood. Although condemned, the woman could hear the sounds of televisions and life coming out the apartments she pass. Peeking through the holes and cracks along the walls on both sides of her, the woman could see people moving and transparent appliances working within some of the rooms. Stopping in front of an apartment with no door, she sees a rather large man choking at a table with two other people. As a middle aged lady smugly plays a hand of cards in front of the severely coughing and wheezing man, he folds over the table and dies. Knowing C.P.R., the woman in the doorway dashes to revive him as the entire room vanishes, leaving an empty, furniture-less space. "O-k, this is crazy." Stopping in her tracks, mesmerized, the woman leaves the apartment in a hurry. Hearing demons move through the other apartments ahead, she manages to pull down part of the already hanging ceiling and grab hold to a portion of protruding frame work. Pulling herself up, she climbs to the next level of corroded wood and joisting. She crawls out the opening of a wall, into what used to be an attic of a remodeled house. Inside a small, dark empty room, she is drawn to the crying of a unseen child. Inching to a corner, she peaks around the turn to an even smaller space and opening of roof. The little girl in the German school dress lay on a patch of old newspapers and clothes, outlined in dead and long dried out stems of flowers. Curled into a ball, the small girl sobbing stops upon the presence of the woman. "What's the matter, why are you crying... and so loudly? The demons will find us, remember?"

"It's okay, I always cry at this time. It was meant." The little girl stare up at her blankly, her eyes grow dark and sickly.

"This time, what do you mean, what time is it? What are you talking about? What are you doing up here by yourself?" The woman scoots in closer to the little girl inside the cramped space. "Do you live here?"

"I'm hiding, the same as you... hiding. I can hide for a long time. Eventually, we all have to come back to our beginning." The girl looks at the woman with tears in her eyes. Her small hands tighten to the bone, as her full oval face thin even more under the shadows, her legs and body shrink into a boney state.

"Wait, where'd you hear that from, who told you that... that crazy old woman? This isn't a good hiding place, those things can get up here!" The woman whispers in concern, "Where are your parents? Why are you always alone?" She stoops down next to the tired and suddenly fatigued acting child. "We need to go."

"I don't always remember things. The longer you stay here, the more you forget." The little girl turns her back to her. "My mother and father told me to hide once... to hide from the men coming." A bright yellow light fills the small space, almost like the Sun shining from a small open window. The woman could see men dressed in suits and old German military hats, standing downstairs through the splitting cracks in the floor. The sounds of heavy boots could suddenly be heard and felt stomping everywhere below them. The little girl's heavy head tilts and falls back, the woman catches and cuffs her bony neck in her hand. "They're soldiers, they never leave. I can hide really good. I can hide without talking for a really long time." The little girl's voice rattles off as she breaks down into bones and dust inside the woman's hand.

"Wait, no... little girl..." The child's small crinkled blue dress flops down loosely over the woman's knees among the dirt and speckles of bone. The yellow light inside the building fades into darkness as the cracks in the floor reseal and repair themselves back into the current flooring beneath her. In emptiness again, the woman realizes that the little girl must have died there, starving and alone. A brief feeling of sorrow overcomes her as she pushes away helplessly, unable to do anything for the deceased child. Glancing down at the tiny legs prints in the dirt that sat just slightly above of the child's tiny shoes, a hot heat blows across her back followed by a vile aroma of sulfur and stench. Whipping around, her eyes meet the beady reds of an enormously horned creature. It's bent, scarred and twisted face, wickedly smiles a long and sharp set of gator like teeth in a fit of revenge. With jealousy and envy towards man, the dark being walks in self-hatred and the immortal curse of banishment. Powerless and ghostly skills un-mastered, the woman scoots deeper into the crevice of roof, cringing at the sheer size of monster.

"Fleeing from your maker is forbidden. Poor pigs, man just can't help but to keep sinning and sinning, even after death. Well wait no longer for your judgement, I will worsen your pain, spawn of Eve." The demons great mouth chomps down, missing her as it tries to squeeze its enormous body around the corner of the small space.

"I'm not running!" The woman screams and kicks at the creature while trying to phase through the wall and floor like the other spirits. The jaws of the demon stretch over the woman, to the ceiling and floor, she accepts her final end. Just before its laughing snout snaps close, the woman hears an old Madame's voice whisper, "Come with me." Letting go, the woman's body is sucked through the floor in a feathery tug, as the teeth of the demon slams shut in thunderous clamp above her. Seeing ceilings, floors and walls, appear and disappear upwards, the woman looks down to see the glowing body of the old woman with the rats and birds pulling her through the rooms of the abandoned building. Twisting upside-down and sideways by the arm, loosely, the woman felt as though she was flying, soaring as free as a bird in the sky. Behind and through the drywall, beneath the floorboards, pass lurking demons and hiding spirits, the woman is taken outside behind the building. In a drizzle of sudden rain, behind two tall cubical trash dumpsters, they gently float down to the sidewalks cold concrete squares.

"Come... stay with me. You are... dead. Come, stay with me." The old woman repeated again, viewing her rotten teeth close to the woman's face. "Never the light."

Looking at all the trash, broken down cardboard boxes about the ground, and the legs of a person still alive, sleeping behind the dumpster, she had a feeling that the old woman dwelt there. "Thankyou, but I can't, I have to..." She could no longer remember what she had to do. But the one thing she knew for sure was that she didn't want to stay there in that place. "I have to go now."

"Come stay with me." The old woman grabs her by both arms as she pulls back. "Don't go into the light, they will eat you." The old woman repeats again as if those were the only words she knew.

"I can't... sorry I can't stay here, I have to take my chances!" The woman snatches away.

"NO!!! you can't hide. Come stay with me!" The old woman hisses as pigeon's pour from underneath her gown and rats scurry from her hair and opens in her clothing. "Stay with me, stay with me, stay with me!" She repeats as a giant six legged demon pounces down onto her from behind a dumpster. The soul of the tattered woman is carried away in the darkness of the night, hollering.

In dismay and shock, the woman dashes off again into the unknown; roaming, lost, scared and confused. Running, the hands of the dead bodies scattered and littered across the ground reanimate, grabbing at her legs and feet. Pulled to the ground, the woman glances around at the demons moving about the shadows in the distance everywhere around her. Forced down, tired, she tries to remember what she was doing there and how she got in the predicament she was in. Unable to remember, she glances down at the bloody holes in her dress, it reminds her of the last seconds with him, her husband. Pushing onward, she breaks and snaps free of the limbs that clasp hold of her. Coming to an alleyway, in the rain, oddly she spots the familiar silhouettes of two men. Moving closer, one of them has a familiar build and the other, an even more familiar face. Slowly approaching them, before she could speak, in a booming sound and burst of amazing bright lights, the man standing next to the more familiarly built fellow falls to the ground dropping a weapon; it was the same man who had shot her. Covering her mouth, the woman glimpse at the black mess of melted goo and dripping substance that cover the back of the head and body of the figure in front of her. Without eyes, nose nor mouth, the dark faceless entity turns to her. Upon its face, a layer of dripping black liquid slowly pour down over a bony skeleton of veiny muscles, like a sheet of thin skin. "You, you bastard, you did this! You took my life! Who are you, why did you do this to us?" The woman cries out, knowing this was the reason she had come and most likely the end of her journey.

"I gave you a chance to join him, you determine where you go. Either way… you cannot run or evade me. I am more than a mere deity. I am a particular part in time, ancient. I am a grim place to some, and a symbol of life to others. What do suppose I am to you?"

As more hands from the petrified bodies rise from the low drifting fog and hold her in place over the cold ground, the woman stares speechlessly into the stone face knowing that of total death. She stares up at the demons behind the buildings and the hundreds of tiny glowing orbs forming around them.

"So, you do know of me? Simple humans, believing they are the center of it all. Know nothing worms, who think they know everything! Tell me, do they still think they are the only ones created in HIS image?" Death laughs and raises its hand. "Foolish man, fearing what they do not know. Cursing me with their pathetic, unjust thinking of how death is the end of it all." In a brilliant beam of energy and light, the woman is raptured by a horde of angelic beings from the sky, Death slowly steps over the body of the man. "Foolish mortals, I am Death, the beginning of a souls eternity." He looks down at the man and vanishes as demons tear the soul of the fallen from its body, hauling it off into the smoking depths of endless darkness with them.

The End

THE 16TH LANDING

A POEM OF THE BEGINNING

Once in a milky way of stars,
far from the center of the universe and space,
there lived a celestial body of peoples
of different colors, intergalactic cultures and race.

The Grays lived amongst the Greens,
between the Nordics of the wilds.
The Silver clan lived on the moons near men,
sharing the land equally with the Reptiles.

And the universe was at peace
and the stars were all aligned.
The eclipse of the Sun marked the
coming of an historical event as
those who stood against peace saw this
as a sign of the end of times.

But in the fear of inducing panic,
the kings declared their fortunes to be locked away,
the leaders covered their finds of their latest discoveries,
insuring it never sees the light of day.
However... unfortunately where ever peace and harmony exist,
evil shall divide.

Over the elapse of time, objects gain
value, resources become power,
as the wicked influence it leaders from
the houses that stand in pride.

The Gray share technology with the people of the water planet,
while the Nordics teach how to nurture the land, to man.
The Reptiles and Silvers who never received assistance,
sneer with jealousy and disgrace, shutting off
all ties beyond all borders of land.

When the Grays couldn't get resources the Nordics left,
and when the Greens began to starve,
they withdrew their great fields of
cultivating stone, flying machines,
and that's what ignited the war.

Man fought against the Reptiles
across the beds of sand,
as the Silvers built a weapon that rained an
ultimate downpour of divine fire,
that singed and burned across the land.

The Grays came down to retrieve what they could
since their moons had been destroyed.
The Reptiles defeated the Silvers great warbirds in the sky.
The remaining Grays release a poison neuro neutralizing gas
that made all the Silvers on the planet of water die.

The Greens, angered by their act, retaliate
by dispersing the most unthinkable, stealthiest
ultra-atomic nuclear, dark matter bomb.
It vanquishes most of solar system
grouped around the Sun.

But somehow the Earth survived, yet, next to
none of the history of the battle is left,
only a faint memory of the lives they lived.
Among the statues, within the carvings of stone and wood,
the untold war lives on, recorded among the pyramids.

-Finis-

THE 17ᵀᴴ LANDING

STALIN'S LADDER

Deep within West Africa's tropical forestry, somewhere deep within the secluded plains between Guinea and Ghana, a secret military base founded by the local government, the Soviet Financial Commission and the Soviet Academy of Sciences, await the arrival of the newest member to its private operations. Hidden from the rest of the world, an underground compound protected by fencing and a hand full of soldier's, operate under the code name, Heaven's Gate. Conducting experiments such as cross breeding, Eugenics, and rejuvenation therapy, the lab (legally disguised as an insemination research facility) also took part in a new underground, government declared Hybridization program designed to benefit humanity and its growing need for organ transplant. Commissioned by several undisclosed institutions to partake in primate testing, the underground centers behavioral and medical experiments set it at the fore front of ground breaking medical discoveries, and advancement in training monkeys for space travel.

Pass a protected biosphere reserve, through saltwater hippo territory, an unmarked, mysterious all terrain military vehicle sped away from a helicopter. Into an old city of Portuguese colonial buildings, across the forested northern belt of the Congo River, the truck drives miles and miles until reaching a rain forest of tree-top canopies and foliage. Stopping at a post guarded by two African men, the vehicle enters an electrical fence. Immediately, the putrid smell of animal feces saturate the air as the primeval sounds of severely tortured children fill the atmosphere. Upon the loud engine of the truck, hundreds of monkeys loudly scatter, vanishing into the trees and wind. Two more guards pull back a wide hanging thick curtain to a large camouflaged tent, the vehicle coast inside as the two men pull the curtains closed behind it. The tent blackens; bright automatic headlights come on. The truck parks directly in front of a mine shaft that plugged into the earth, in the middle of three tables of monitors, mostly covered by large table clothes. Four boots step out of the truck; heavy doors riddled in bullet holes and dents slam beside them.

"Welcome to your new home, doctor." St. Clair Julius Washington, a veterinarian, surgeon, computer analyst and programmer, spoke in a deep voice. A medium height, nicely groomed black man with a low cut fade, stood in military gear and hat. He straightens his shirt and walks to the back of the truck to retrieve some equipment. "Grab your things."

"Seriously, you're joking right?" Richard Adler, a well-known geneticists and neurosurgeon, lunges two large duffel bags over his thin shoulders and steps over to the hole dug in front of the truck. "Let me get this straight, we're going to fit all of this... down that man sized hole?" Richard thought about the computers he still had left in the truck.

St. Clair struts over to a set of uncovered computers sitting on a table and enters a five digit code; an elevator rises from the floor beneath the hole. "Gets em every time." He snickers as two large elevator doors open up in front of them.

"Wow. Is it really like the Professor says?" Richard, Sandy haired, cleaned shaved with glasses, looks at his old college with great trust before entering.

"And more... let's just say, so far, from what I've seen, it's definitely an upgrade from the last hole in the wall we worked in." St, Clair watches Richard carry his bags inside. "We'll come back for the rest."

"Why are you dressed like that?" Richard blurts out.

"Like what?"

"Like... them?"

"Camouflaged? It helps me to blend in. Look, this is the only time we're going to get to go outside for a long time. I hope you enjoyed your time out." St. Clair smiles, pressing the button to close the elevator doors. The quaint compartment slid horizontally downward, lowering miles deep inside the shaft. Smelling of hot plastic, gear grease and metal, the elevator, already entrapping the hot heat and wild smells from outside, journey far below the surface to the lower levels of a hidden facility. Richard Adler glances at the five levels numbered downward, highlighted upon the panel of the elevator. The sweat box stops on the second level, opening to a gust of cool air.

"Feels good in here." Pouring of sweat, Richard embraces the air conditioning of the central air units. "Who'd ever think we'd come this far?" He admires the large, bright space.

"We're in the living quarters. We'll detour through the kitchen then I'll show you to your room." St. Clair leads him down a dimly lit hall of tinted glass doors. Just ahead, they hear muffled sounds coming through the walls. "We're in the east wing, your room is in the west wing."

"I hear talking. Is everyone here?" Richard quickly strokes his fingers through his damp head; his legs buckled underneath the weight of the heavy duffel bags on his back.

"Yep... to my knowledge. But who knows for sure what surprise guest the Professor might have for us. He's known for that, you know?" St. Clair swings a badge that hung from a thin chain on his neck across a computerized panel on a door. It opens into a large kitchen and dining area occupied by a large table full of food and members of the crew.

"Ah, St. Clair, you return, and you've brought our missing comrade, Dr. Adler, just in time! Now our family is once again completed!" Professor Boris Vadim Kazimir, an elderly man from

Moscow, spoke with a strong accent. "Drop your things, you're just in time for dinner and a toast! St. Clair and the others will help you get settled in a moment. For now, we drink and give thanks! Go on, sit your things down, quickly. St. Clair, you can sit the terminals down on the counter top for now? Thankyou." Sexologist, geneticists, neurosurgeon, head scientist and director of the institute, the Professor; tall and in great shape for the age of 63, takes hold of his glass of wine and wait for the others.

"Richard, you made it!" The warm and cheery voice of Abigail Lapin, a zoologist and primatologist greets him from the opposite side of the large table. With her long dark hair pulled back in a ponytail, in a white, buttoned up, short sleeve shirt and jeans, her small hourglass frame leans against the table. Throughout the years of working on and off, she had gained a undisclosed sweet spot for him.

"Abigail, it's good to..." Richard stares at her beautiful dark eyes and petite pink lips.

"Hello Rich." Douglas Sasson, a computer wizard, engineer and the hands on camera man, interrupts. "Glad you could join us bro." He speaks in a condescending tone. Patting Richard on the shoulder, he smears crumb cake on his back. Rejoining the table, Douglas dust the crumbs off his black goal-tee with a napkin. Young with black gelled hair, he smirks and cuts his sneaky eyes across the room.

"Yeah, we thought you weren't going to make it back this time. Nice to see you Richard." Nikita Ho Chi Minh, a short and spunky Asian woman spoke. With her long, fine black hair pulled into a bun, she poses a nice frail frame in jeans and a white button shirt. A veterinarian and neurosurgeon from China, she runs up and hugs her friend whom she haven't seen in nearly a year. "Somebody misses you." She raises her brow at Abigail across the table and steps away.

"Douglas, Nikita." Richard greets them both. Unable to take

his eyes off of Abigail, whom he had not seen for some time; he tucks his two large army bags together at his feet.

"I'm glad you returned to us safely, I was beginning to worry. How were the labs at C.M.G.H.? [Cleveland Metropolitan General Hospital]" Abigail pulls a couple of bobby pins from her head, releasing a free flowing body of long, graying and curly brown hair that fell to her shoulders.

"It was great! A little repetitious and tedious but... I'll live. It was a wonderful experience but like the old saying goes... there's no place like home. I missed you guys." Richard responds as Professor Kazimir clangs a silver spoon against his half full glass of champagne. Richard glances over at a unfamiliar looking, young, disabled gentlemen sitting in a wheelchair next to the Professor.

"Attention, attention everyone, all ladies and gents alike! I'm going to make this fast, so Mr. Adler and the rest of you can get settled in and reacquainted." The Professor silences the room. "Welcome, welcome back to our new home. This is Will, our guess from outside. He will be spending the night with us as we prepare our new facility. I've invited him to come and keep an eye on us since science... is his favorite thing. Right, Will?" Professor Kazimir smiles down at the young man visiting from an unknown medical center. "As you can see, we are bigger, better, stronger, and now have access to unlimited resources. There is nothing we won't be able to achieve nor do and now... we have no need to answer to anyone! No longer will our decisions be challenged by outside parties. Everything we say and do will strictly be confidential and confined within this facility until we decide to release the information or otherwise. This time around, we will undergo multiple experiments and partake in a range of projects that will require monotonous multitasking. That is why I have summoned you here! You are the best of the best and have been the most loyal to me and my work in the past. I thank each of you for that. And for your dedication to years of service, I have granted you full access to your own labs and studios, so you can also create your own projects that I know will be an asset to the company. Here, we will give our life to science, here, we will do everything we can to benefit humanity. Welcome to Heaven's Gate! To the future of scientific discovery!" Professor Kazimir tips his glass, toasting to the room as they cheer to his speech.

"Professor, how'd you do it? This is wonderful, how did you get the ventilators and... approval for the MRI machines alone? We must've been funded millions for this?" Abigail smiles curiously, overwhelmed by their new facility.

"Through long and gruesome political begging my dear." The Professor laughs. Taking a sip of his glass, he strokes his graying beard and eyes Douglas who just nibbled off a saucer of more cake, watching. "Seriously, I promise you, it was a hard process, but finally we have everything we need to be successfully productive. Nikita, show our friend Will here, the cake, please?" He kindly ask the scientist.

"Professor Kazimir, I couldn't help but notice all the chimps running around outside. Are they protected?" Nikita ask, taking a seat over a plate of fish and pasta. Enthusiastically, her beautifully dark, slanted eyes stare across the table of food.

"Yes, but... a good deal has been made with the local community. Some of them are tagged and belong to our own institution. This time, with our combined software and equipment, we will be able to do the tasks of a hundred man crew." The Professor glances down at his empty glass. "Like I said before, here... we will give our life to science, remember that."

Listening closely to the Professors words, Richard Adler peers over at St. Clair and Abigail; anxiously ready to tour the facility.

CHAPTER 1

THE COMPOUND

Starting from the 1st level, which was mainly filled with computers, lounge areas and office space, Douglas Sasson and the Professor, shows the crew around the facility. Down long halls of transparent glass windows and tiled floors, the crew come to two security booths guarded by two African men. As one soldier sat in front of a monitor at a desk inside the booth on the left, another stood between the booths at the foot of the walkway. The professor nods a partial smile at the soldier who still eyes the crews clothing for i-d's anyway. Remembering their faces, the guard nods back at the Professor, allowing them to pass.

"Wow, we're working with the military now?" Whispers Richard Adler.

"Dr. Adler, we're at a new level of operations. Isn't it nice to finally have some outside cooperation?" Professor Kazimir whispers back between the inert silver material visibly wedged in the throbbing, freshly done, root canal of his teeth. He holds his head in a smug manor.

"Professor, you sure got a lot of people on the pay role this time." St. Clair Jullius Washington admires, thinking of the hand full of scattered military people he's been observing around building in the last few days. Richard eyes Abigail Lapin inquisitively.

Down a lengthy stretch of concrete walls, ceilings and flooring, the group come to a large automated fence. Behind the fence was a deep tunnel that extended miles and miles back to the surface somewhere close to the open road.

"As you can see, much of this floor is used for storage. Beyond this door are the docks by which we ship, receive and use to transport our patients." The Professor addresses, dressed in black slacks, a white shirt, black tie and lab coat. The gates opens. Startling the group; three solders escort a forklift with huge teeth, carrying a metal cage with breathing holes directly by them. As the professor rubs his hand against the passing container, loud bangs and knocks, followed by growls, explode from inside the box. The wretched noise echo and bounce down the empty halls of the tunnel, dampening the native thoughts and spirits of any African soldier hearing it. The container sways and rocks, as impressions are indented from the inside out and knocked across the outside body of the container; indicating that whatever was on the inside, wanted desperately to get out. The remaining crew move close to St. Clair; Douglas laughs behind them, excited by the sounds and quite intrigued with what might actually be inside the container. "Ah, one of our patients now! Returning from recreational exercising I presume, good." Professor Kazimir salutes the men, watching them escort the cage through a set of large swinging doors.

"Professor, you never told me exactly what it was we would be specifically working on. What exactly… is my role here?" St. Clair asked, still hearing the shuttering sounds of the cage, loudly in the back of his mind. He wanted to make sure that he wouldn't be working with whatever it was screaming inside that container.

"Um, you didn't tell me either!" Nikita Ho Chi Minh adds as Richard and Abigail agree as well.

"Science my friends, science. That is all we will be…" He glances over them confidently and suddenly stares off into his walky-talky radio, disturbed. "Douglas, take over for me. I need to attend to one of our patients. I have to make sure our matters are in order at all times, excuse me." The Professor leaves the party and walks off quickly towards the double doors. "Make sure to get plenty of rest, we have no time to waste! We start first thing in the morning!" He speaks loudly, sliding his badge across a panel that protruded from a post on the floor. Exiting abruptly, he leaves the crew oddly standing silently in the hall.

Loading onto another elevator near the center of the underground building, the group of scientist and computer techs pass back through the second level, named the Galley, which was the kitchen and living quarters they began in. Downward onto the third level, a much cooler floor, the doors of the elevators open into a long hall of steel mobile beds, medical equipment and devices. Going through a set of doors, they enter an even larger white room. Counters aligning the walls, St. Clair and Richard touch and rub their hands across table topped cabinets that automatically raise out the floor upon entry. From the center of the area the party overlooks other small laboratories of military workers connected to the outskirts of the room.

"Welcome to Gemini." Douglas Sasson introduces, spinning around in a slow circle. "Nikita baby, this is the floor you'll mainly be working on." He informs her as everyone in the group scatter and walk around, peeping into the windows of each lab. "Everyone will have their own assistant. So no fighting over help."

A hand full of military men and women attended to the maintenance of equipment while others helped in caring for test specimens. Mice and a variety of rodents scurry about their own plastic cages, energetically running around on their 0wheels to nowhere, as dogs of all sort, bark, quiver, and sniff about their cages inside separate labs.

"Are those dogs? What are we going to be doing with dogs?" Richard whispers to Nikita, walking up to a large double room with tinted windows, sitting in the furthest corner of the storage area.

"What's in there?" Abigail ask, "Why are the windows tinted?"

"Top secret, guess you'll have to find that out when the good ol Professor let you inside. But if I was to guess, I'd say it's for the security measures." Douglas annoyingly chews on a toothpick. "Everything's not for public eyes, remember? You know how private the Professor is about some of his... work." He lightly huffs under his breath and turns away. "As you can see, all animal testing and transplant operations will be done here."

"Wait, these can't be what I think they are? No way!" Richard examines a grouping of small portable machines. "They're so small, they have to be... because I can see the... are these miniature Excimer Laser systems?" He becomes excited and then curious about the usage of such machines.

"Yep, the big daddies are in the labs." Douglas answers, walking back to the exit.

"We're able to perform laser surgery? Cool." Nikita comments as St. Clair looks down at her. She waves at an African woman behind the glass.

"Yeah, but on what? I hope we're not back to... mmmmm." St. Clair grumbles, keeping his comment to himself.

"Come on, let's mosey on downstairs, kiddies! To the fourth floor, follow me!" Douglas instructs, guiding them to the door. As the crew overlooks the floor one last time, he watches one of the Military scientist give a mouse a shot through one of the glass windows. Taking them to the next level, slightly less lit and emptier than the Gemini, the computer tech welcomes the group to a quiet intersection of halls and empty labs filled with unmanned machinery. "Ladies and gentlemen, I present... the Ovich 1!" Douglas spins out the elevator and provides access to the door on the right. Into a room of sinks and cabinets, he leads them through a set of double doors as if they were about to perform surgery on a patient. "We're still stocking equipment. So, as you can see, this will also become part of your daily responsibilities as a member of the Professors special family." Douglas rolls his eyes at Abigail and peers off devilishly.

As Richard enters what appears to be some sort of large

operating room, he eyes Catheters, Needle-less syringes and Sperm separators, boxed upon the cabinets and counter tops. "This is an insemination lab!"

"Correct, we're inside the hybridization chamber. The Professor wanted to be the one to expose you to all of this, but, as you can see, he's a busy man. I'm sure he'll brief you more in depth later. But this is it, this is where most of the magic will be happening." He guides them pass beds constructed of hi-tech restraints and larger than life sized containment devices.

"Inseminating chimps? What on earth... kind of chimp is going in that thing?" Nikita whispers to St. Clair as they continue into a connecting room.

Crossing paths with more monitors, racks of blood pumps, oxygenating and feeding units, Richard glimpse at Abigail and stares at Douglas. "Uh... I'm not the smartest guy in the world but..." He leans against the back of a wheel chair and touches a table of bizarre surgical cutting tools. "Those look like tanks against the wall? Tanks used for...extracorporeal hypothermic perfusion? Freezing brains?" Richard rubs his head in disbelief.

"Oh my goodness, we're going to be transferring brains? Chimp brains!" Abigail uses context clues and puts two and two together. "Can we even do that now? Is that even legal?"

"Possible, it's already been done. We're just improving on the methods and finalizing their findings." Answers Douglas.

"In other words, copy-catting insanity." St, Clair mumbles under his breathe. "What did I sign up for?"

"This is the end of the tour, tomorrow, it begins!" Douglas rushes them.

"Wait, there are five levels, we've only been to four. What's below us?" Nikita interrupts.

"Level five... Sukhumi, is unauthorized at this time. That's where we store, I mean keep our patients. It's also where we test our subjects IQ and train them for space flight. That's where the Professors at right now, we have a new shipment that just came in. But you'll visit in due time, some of us will be working there as well." Douglas explains, spinning a key chain of keys and pass cards in his hand.

"Why we're we not explained all of this? I just don't understand why we weren't informed of what we were going to be involved in over the phone? Why such a hush, hush?" Abigail blurts out.

"Well... he handpicked us, he's paying us handsomely, and you have benefits and unlimited access to your scientific desires... maybe he knew you wouldn't come? You all are free to leave at any time today if you have a change of heart. As a matter of fact, you probably shouldn't be here now if you're not staying. I've been working hard for this, and I know you have too. I need this... you, you can go home if you don't want it. Work begins tomorrow. Begin learning your way around." Douglas leaves the room as if angered by their questions.

"Can't wait." St. Clair folds his arms and moves next to Nikita.

"This is going to get very interesting." Richard stares down at a bed with some sort of head clamp attached to it.

CHAPTER 2

THE EXPERIMENTS

The following morning and day of preparations came quickly; launching into bold weeks of setting up, months of test trials until finally reaching full operations, Heaven's Gate, is a go. Assisted by the military, inside a small lab within the Gemini, Professor Kizimir, Nikita Ho Chi Minh, Richard Adler, and Douglas Sasson, perform a very unique surgery on mice. Dabbling in a few experiments of artificially growing human and synthetic tissue onto organic life, the scientist, under the helm of the professor, swiftly transcend to bigger experiments. Monitors, connected to a host of computers, wires and other devices, emit measurements of pressure and diagnostic readings from upon a small table of scientific surgeons. Beeping sounds and the shifting of both soft soled and dress shoes alike, blended over talking and the hard clicking of fingers against a plastic key pad. Under bright ceiling lights that illuminated the dim room, anticipation and anxiety grow among the scientist dressed in blue surgeon clothes, gloves, hair covers and face mask.

"Respiratory system is normal." Nikita calls out, standing over the table next to two African women, one holding small vials of blood and the other, disposable needles. Uncomfortably warm, she glances at numbers fluctuating on a small screen. "She's breathing fine. There doesn't seem to be any oxygen lost."

"No misfires in the brain either, all activities appear normal." Richard adds, double-checking the computer. "This is amazing!"

"We have about a minute before it awakes, finish unplugging it." Professor Kizimir lowers a lamp down from the ceiling as Douglas maneuvers around them, filming the entire scene on camera. "Beautiful, perfect." The professor smiles from behind his thin framed glasses.

Disconnected from wires that ran to a heart monitor, and from others connected to various medical machines, an adult, shaved, white rat opens its beady red eyes on the center of a small operating table. Extremely groggy, yet fully functional, it twitches its long tiny whiskers and sniffs the wind; unaware of the two infant heads of mice, grafted onto each of its thighs.

"Four weeks and the infant brains are still developing. The brain cooling test was a success!" Richard Adler sighs in relief. Turning around, he looks at their previous test subjects caged inside hi-tech glass enclosures within the walls behind him. "Incredible." His eyes scroll pass the guinea pigs and selection of mixed crossbred rodents, to a mouse hooked up to a ventilator. White bodied, an unmatched black head of another mouse, swapped with the original rodent's head, fights to breathe while pumping blood on its own into its new heart. Then slowly drifting to the sight of larger cages, Richard slightly becomes uneasy by the sight of sickly dogs with two heads, both able to move and drink water. But the one that bothered his conscience the most was Hagar and Tuni, two canines bred in labs with the upper bodies of younger dogs grafted onto their shoulders. Living over a month, barking and alert, the attentive heads and front legs of pups drape over the necks of the two large adult males.

"The medicine really helps prevent rejection by the immune system. Oh the spoils we're going to reap from this research! I think we're ready for the next phase." Professor Kazimir stands upright as one of the assistants dabs his face with a paper towel. "I think we're highly capable of keeping the brain alive while out of its own body. Have you taken a look at patient 20? Its brain shows EEG [echoencephalograph] activity and has been taking up oxygen and glucose."

"Really?" Richard Adler walks over to a large glass window shielding a metal, cylindrical chamber attached to tubes and monitors. Peering at a chart hanging off a small ledge going around the containment, he glances down at a dog laying unconscious on a bed, strapped down to devices. It had the brain of another dog transplanted in its neck.

"We're making real head way. Several human diseases without cures could benefit from this. I'm down for a cephalic exchange!" Nikita seals the enclosure around the lab rat.

"Whoa, hold your horses. Are you guys listening to what you're saying? The next level, I can only imagine what that is." Richard sarcastically comments. "This is fantastic, but I need time to process this! We're moving incredibly fast."

"Dr. Adler, we have no time to waste. We must continue one hundred percent forward. We've redefined hypothermic perfusion my boy. You and Nikita see what we have achieved, you now see the path we're on. You see patient 12?" He points to the mouse with the black head and large white body. "Just the tip of the ice berg. Richard, I want you to help me perform a cephalosomatic anastomosis."

"Lucky!" Nikita freezes in place to listen. "Wow!"

"What, a Cephaloso... on what, a mouse? Ha!" Richard laughs as Doug walks between them making ape sounds. "No... really? Is that what you want to do with the chimps? Surgically transfer their heads? I... I thought we were helping to breed them? Helping to save an endangered species? I don't think we're ready for this. What if we're moving too fast? You're talking about spinal reconnection and possible abuse." Richard remembers that an outside company was present among them, the military. "We could accidentally kill a lot of animals Professor." He continues anyway, yet still lowering his voice.

"Many could benefit from the study alone, and it's all cleared.

Why not, this is what we're here for isn't it? Richard? Here, we give our lives to science, remember?" Professor Kazimir reminds him.

"We all have to die sometimes, right?" Douglas snickers back by them again, shutting down his camera.

His comment draws Richard's attention back to patient 12, the plump white rodent switched with another rats head. Noticing the rat suffocating on its own fluids, connected to a small respirator, it stops breathing and dies in its container before he could reach it.

"Professor, sorry to interrupt, but we have a problem in the cage." Babak, a 5ft 7, African man dressed in a high ranking military uniform, storms into the lab.

"Huh... at this time?" Professor Kazimir huffs, surprised by the Guard. "Figures. Richard, we'll discuss this at a later time. Excuse me." The Professor takes off his gloves and pulls down his mask. "Oh, and by the way; this is Babak, he's in charge of all our extra hands around here. Get used to him. Mrs. Ho Chi Minh, great work. What's the matter, are the intercoms not working? It is insanitary for you to be in here my friend, this mistake must not happen again. But do to the severity of the situation, I..."

"Professor, he should come as well." Babak glimpses sternly at Douglas, who was transferring the footage from the cameras along the ceiling onto disc.

"Who, Douglas? Oh, well of course. Come Douglas, your help is always needed as well, apparently." The Professor instructs, exiting to the scrub room. As Babak walks out the unauthorized security door which he came from, Douglas tosses his gloves into a wastebasket and joins him. Richard and Nikita stands behind in the laboratory with the two military aids, lost in thought.

IVAN

A gloomy evening brings the coastal region its tropical six month rain as a sudden downpour beat against the earth on top of the secret underground lair. Professor Kazimir and the other scientist continue to search for a solution to sustain a human after the body has been sacrificed. Away from prying eyes, scientist could freely search for the secrets to prolonging life. Partaking in more controlled experiments such as grafting body parts, and the transplanting of hearts and lungs, the scientist began practicing attaching arteries to the body of dogs, and redirecting the flow of blood between the decapitated heads they grafted onto animals. Thus, studying certain problems of the nervous system, brain activity and the relationship between the cortex and sub-cortex. Many test were carried out on animals and organs removed from their corpses and kept alive by machines. At first, only giving the subjects connected to a machine a ten minute life span, Professor Kazimir, and his unorthodox methods extended the life cycles by days, weeks and months. Swapping the heads of mice, they learned that by keeping the donors brain stem, the body is able to continue to control its own heartbeat and breathing. And as their knowledge in surgical neurology increased, the Professor and his team attempts one final preliminary experiment before the next phase of their plight.

"Gauze, remove the pins. Julienne, give me two more electrodes, carefully. Record the waves on the EEG (electroencephalogram), Richard. Ah that's it, thank you Abigail." Nine hours after a long surgery, the Professor and his sought out, multi-skilled surgeons stand over a hospital bed along with two helping hands from the military, Julienne and Hannatu. "Look at our work ladies and gentlemen, subject B is a success." Professor Kazimir, sweating, stares down at their latest patient. Having transplanted the entire head of an imported rhesus monkey onto the body of another, Professor Kazimir marvels at a paralyzed monkey laying in the hospital bed.

Without its spinal chord fused, the brown mangy monkey, still, after having its head transferred from its old body to a new, opens its eyes for the first time. Focusing, its large pupils began to dart frantically across the room. "Good, the anesthesia is wearing off." The Professor watches Abigail Lapin check its vision.

"Eye sights normal. Seems to be able to see." She shines a bright light into the primate's groggy eyes, then checks its heart and blood pressure.

Professor Kazimir snaps his fingers next to the monkey's ears, "Bell." He rings a small bell on both sides of the monkeys head and rubs a small pointy rod around the inside and outside of the monkey's ears. "It can hear as well." Poking a small slender rod around its face, he admires the primate's facial responses. He had once again proven that an animal could survive without suffering brain injury.

"A few more test should do it. Cross-circulation and hypothermia are very effective neuroprotective strategies." Richard stands across from him at a monitor attached to the bed. "Amazing, at the rate we're going we'll be able to help disabled people in no time." Hannatu places dirty surgical tools on a tray next to him.

"To save paraplegics would be a dream come true." The Professors eyes squint behind his surgeon mask, indicating he was smiling. "Enough spinal chord left intact could allow for a successful head transplant. In theory, they could regain full use of a donor's body. Patients with muscular dystrophy could receive completely new lives, second chances." Watching the rhesus monkey, he could tell that the monkey did not want to be there at all. The Professor smiles as if he was looking down at a newborn baby.

"It's already been tried and can't be done. Besides, were talking years down the road for this technology." Abigail looks down sadly at the twitching face of the primate, checking the staples around its neck and shoulders.

Laying on the table in head clamps, body restraints, connecting tubes and sensors, the rhesus monkey, having been captured in the wilderness and operated on, stares around a strange and new alien environment. Becoming agitated with the constant jabbing and non-movement of its own body, it is partially calmed by the professor shoving small berries and tasty treats into its mouth. Irritably feeding, its frightened, weary eyes peer at Abigail and two military assistants beside her from West Africa. Unable to utter a sound in defiance, the monkey begins fighting against the Professors hand, pushing the food out of its mouth with its tongue. It tries to bite his hand.

"It can taste as well." A hint of extra enthusiasm touches Kazimir's voice. "Haven't our experiments on the mice taught us anything? We were able to restore connectivity between two severed halves of the spinal cords! Any things possible." Exclaims the professor, he stands and takes off his gloves. "Hannatu, take over. Same as we discussed."

"I think it's fantastic." Douglas controls a overhanging camera from a small touch screen monitor connected to his laptop; he zooms in closer onto the table. "We're at the top of our game, we're going to be millionaires!" He laughs happily from a nearby table.

"There's nothing fantastic about not being able to move your body or someone else's." Groaned Abigail, checking the primate's heart and blood pressure. "No visible ruptures, temperature and vital signs good."

"Nothing fantastic... are you kidding me? You don't even know what you're talking about! This is the only treatment that could possibly work on paralyzed patients. Gene therapy has failed! Wait until we attach the spinal chord, you're talking about spine regeneration!" Douglas becomes upset. "I'd say we're on the verge of saving life!"

"And what would you know about that? You're not a surgeon, you're only in this for a paycheck!" Abigail slams a stethoscope down on a metal tray causing Richard to key in repeating letters on the keypad of the computer.

"Douglas! Go assist St. Clair in the cage. We're done here for the evening." Professor Kazimir orders; breaking up the potential growth of an argument. Douglas places the cameras on his automatic settings and storms out the laboratory. He gazes at the cages of experimental mice that aligned the wall in numerous transparent cells behind them and flicks one with his fingers. One mouse, its head transferred to a new body and spine reattached, squirms and crawls on two impaired, bent front legs to a small block of yellow cheese. It erratically twitches and nervously tries to control its own direction, swiveling in circles before sniffing and nibbling off a tiny piece. "We are close to developing a new technology Mrs. Lapin. We cannot be afraid to take things to higher levels. I believe we are closer to the next step in evolution and I want you on board Abigail, you too Richard. I have developed two new procedures, one that will heal the spinal column faster and another that will successfully preserve the brain, so that it too can be transplanted without a skeleton. This is just the breaking of the ice, I tell you. It is time for us to begin human testing." He takes off his mask, strokes his white beard and rubs his scruffy face.

"Human testing? Now wait a minute, are you serious? He's serious. How, what medical grounds do you have for doing such an experiment? And even if we had the capability, where on earth would you get a volunteer for such a thing? How can you be able to regenerate the nerves which produce that sort of control?" Richard drops everything and peers dumbfounded at Abigail. "I, I just think it's way too soon for that sort of test trial and those sorts of conclusions!"

"Boris, listen to what you're saying." Abigail addresses the professor by his first name. "What you're proposing is unethical. Monkeys are one thing, human testing is another. We could be sued and worse yet, people could die!" She raises her concerns. Glimpsing at all the experimental animals caged around them, she began to question the professor's real motives in the back of her mind. Douglas eavesdrop from the shadows of the next room; he sneaks away quietly in the darkness.

"Like I said; our resources now are unlimited. We can do whatever we feel necessary or deem fitting to our project. My plan; I say first we start with cadavers, and then we take volunteers. It won't be that difficult. I have checked both of your files, even you have signed to be an organ donor when you die. Each of you! Now imagine how many people we'd find in the public sector?" Professor Kazimir peers over the glasses fallen to the tip of his nose, and slicks down what was left of his balding, wild standing gray hair. "Look, this procedure could be used to treat the paralyzed and people unable to move their limbs. People whose bodies were diseased, rather than their brains, could be linked to entirely new bodies. Already we have transported the brain as a separate organ into an intact animal and maintained it viable from many days. Together, we have retrained the brain in the skull. Paraplegics with certain injuries could regain full usage of a donor's body. It's all about the betterment of mankind."

"No, I… can't, its morally wrong." Abigail thinks about the opportunity she was about to pass up and the grounds by which she could possibly get fired. She holds out her hands as one of their assistants removes her gloves. "I… I can't join you in that experiment Professor. You're playing with the very essence of life, you don't know what part of the body the soul is stored. What if the patients worse off in the end? I can't."

"I think the usage of cadavers is a weird but… a great start. We would just need a fresh body. I could handle that. But live patients… the disabled? I dunno Professor, I think it's way too risky to be trying these operations on people. The risk of bad just doesn't quite outweigh the risk of success." Richard closes out the menu on the monitor and restores the computers system to its preset diagnostic settings.

"But how do you know if something works if you never try to bring the idea to life?" Professor Kazimir spins around to them. "We could use spinal chord stimulation and other techniques to aid in spinal recovery. Along with my methods, a negative pressure device will create a vacuum and encourage the nerves to fuse faster and more naturally."

"And what is this magical method you're using to repair the spinal chord?" Questions Richard.

"You must be on board to reach that destination, Richard." Kazmir takes off his glasses and smirks. Richard and Abigail pause in silence.

"Why does it sound like you've already done this?" Abigail mutters under her breath, then glimpse at Kazimir's non-joking, flushed face.

Stepping a few feet away to a solid black, reflective wall between the shelving of contained lab mice, Professor Kazimir raises his identification badge and swipes it across a hidden panel. The wall; which was actually another glass door, opens into an even more elaborate laboratory. "Hannatu, Julienne, cover us. Finish connecting the electrodes and monitor its electrical activity. You two, come with me." He signals Richard Adler and Abigail Lapin to accompany him. Entering the bizarre room of more workers, and sick, dead, and dying bed ridden experimental Chimps, he walks them over to a section of twisted, contorted mice with their necks and backs shaved and stitched. Three military assistants already occupying the room before they entered, nod at their presence. As some of the rodents bend in spasms of pain inside rows of open containers, on what looked like a line of silver platters, lay the heads of dogs, monkeys and organs; each kept alive by an array of unique machines and pumps.

"What, how?" Unable to get out his words, Richard enters the unknown lab, speechless at what he was seeing. "How long have you been doing this?"

"How were you able to achieve this without us? I thought we were the only team here?" Abigail stares around the room at endless incomplete and failed experiments.

"I never said you were the only team." Professor Kazimir smiles and gives them a reassuring wink. He walks over to a table with the head of a monkey suspended over a metal tray; clamped and supported on a post. As Richard and Abigail moves in closer, an elaborate artificial subarachnoid hypothermic perfusion machine clicks on a venous and arterial pump connected to the head. A flow of recycled blood is pumped back into the dome of the chimp, its face begins twitching and eyes start moving under its eyelids. "See this room right here? These are my prize possessions, and the living proof of my testament. They're what started it all." He points around the room. "This is Ivan. Although a chimps head, he's no ordinary monkey. He's very important and very dear to me indeed."

Richard observes the chimp's bald head and traces of stitches encircling underneath the electrodes stuck to its temple as well. "What's wrong with it?"

"Nothing. This head was passed onto me by another researcher over ten years ago. Inside Ivan's head is a living human brain of someone from the nineteenth century. No one knows for certain how many times it's been removed and transplanted out but, Ivan's mind is over sixty years old." Kazimir softly strokes the chimp's hair as blood quickly flows back into the head; the chimp frowns and eyes slowly open, adjusting to the brightness of the light. "The brain lives and yet the isolated head still reacts to external stimuli, light and sound." He takes a feather, tickles its face and knocks against the surface of the tray the head rested on. The monkey's startled reaction sends chills through Abigail's spine. "Every time he expires, my machine revives him within ten minutes."

Still oddly fascinated, Abigail looks around at the all the beating and pumping isolated kidneys, hearts and lungs around the room, attached to many artificial circulating systems, ranging in multiple shapes and sizes. Watching blood pump into a hearts cardiovascular system, her eyes wonder across to an area of brains. "This is... this is... wow! Are there other labs here that we don't know about as well?"

"A few." Professor Kazimir scratches the chin of the monkey with wiggling fingers as if it were a dog.

"No, it's impossible. This is amazingly unreal! You're telling me that you kept a brain alive for over a decade? Impossible. And it has been transplanted multiple times? Professor, who's leg are you pulling here? And what kinds of medical secrets are we really withholding?" Richard laughs jokingly, yet serious about the matter.

"Look at this, there are so many." Abigail identifies dead organs and animals.

"Mr. Adler, must I reveal all my secrets? I assure you, it's all legitimate. Neuroscience has helped to save countless human lives, even if it does kill lots of dogs and monkeys along the way." Kazimir's strong animalistic eyes peer at Abigail from underneath his bushy brows. "But as to your question, yes, what can I say? I have a recipe that works. The magical word here is… Perfusion! With the proper combination of ingredients, ACSF (artificial cerebrospinal fluid) and the right circulatory technology, I have sustained the lifespan of the isolated brain and organ without any severe tissue or nerve damage." He walks over taps on a glass container of dark red liquid, proudly. "However, some live and some die in the process. It's the nature of everything, but… it all started with Ivan. Through developing ways to preserve him, all of this happened."

"This happened? You said your friend Ivan here, really has a human brain inside it, which makes it human. Do you think the person who that brain belongs to is happy? I mean, you say it's aware, could it possibly still be thinking human thoughts?" Abigail shakes her head with an even greater concern. "Boris, were going to fall into a trap of desperately trying to keep people alive using people, its misguided. And if this works, who determines who's life gets to be prolonged? Who will it be, just the important people, the rich?"

"Professor, we know where you trying to go with this. You're talking about fundamentally compromising the body in a whole new way? We're not ready for human experimentation." Richard looks the old scientist directly in his disappointed eyes firmly.

Professor Kazimir looks down at his feet with guilt, then raises his head. "We have already begun."

Down stairs below, deep within the fifth sub-level of the facility, the potent smell of animal feces blows across a stained concrete floor. From inside the basement of the building, howls dozens of chimpanzees. Cage after cage of distraught looking monkeys come into view, gnawing at the bars and scampering around their enclosures. St. Clair, monitoring how well the monkeys were being kept in captivity, overlooks The Cage; the living quarters of the chimpanzees. In the middle of the floor, he struts between stacked cages that connected small pathways to a large open, active primate habitat. Beyond the open gates of the chimp's individual cells, the small passageways guided the animals into a miles high, slightly wider than a football field, enclosed area. Watching a few chimps who were freshly caught in the wild, play and interact with each other, St Clair takes a head count and checks the food of two military aides who were feeding a group of chimps separated from the others. Adapting to multitasking throughout the building, St. Clair, having taking on responsibilities of prepping the primates for testing and various experiments, start to become quite comfortable and attached to the small apes. Helping to feed, clean after and care for the chimps day after day, their captivity began to slowly eat away at his conscience. Standing in the front of the cage belonging to a newer chimp nick named Hugo, St Clair observes the chimp howling out for its family and pacing the floor of its cage agitated. Trying to calm the chimp with sounds, gentle words and a pale of food, St. Clair connects with the pain of separation and anxiety clearly illustrated within the actions of the chimp. Thinking of what will happen to the monkey sometime soon down the line, his spirits sadden and attitude towards the chimps soften even more. St. Clair is instantly reminded of his ancestors past, slavery and history of the cruel treatment towards African Americans; he stops to take a breather.

"How are you doing, my brother?" A deep voice startles him. "Caring for the chimps isn't as easy of a task as one may think, is it?" Babak, Military Commander and man in charge of all the extra persons in the building, asks. Checking on the progress of his people, he walks up on St. Clair from behind. "How are they today?" His multi-colored green, faded camouflage gear clung tightly to his broad muscular body, expanding wide, with each of his slow breaths. Stubbed face, the exposed portions of his clean dark brown bald head shine under the ceiling lights as three rolls of neck fat stacked upon the back of his shirt collar. Babak's presence alone, stood out like an old war veteran, still ready for combat.

"Good, actually. Just a little concerned about how the new addition is going to get along with the chimps we already caught." St. Clair replies looking down at his clipboard of papers.

"Well I don't think you have to worry much about that. All the monkeys are from the same area and family. Once he regroups with the others, I'm sure he'll regain some security. You know, they are very complex creatures. Much like men." Babak reassures him, while also hinting on his expertise in the chimpanzee culture. "What do you see when you gaze into their eyes? Friends, family, a soul?" He looks away towards the crew going on break.

"Pain." St. Clair looks into the face of a caged chimp. A series of newly formed wrinkles within the chimp's forehead suggested a reasoned thought, and how it studied him as it moved from all fours to two legs, back and forth about its cage, illustrated a concept of self thought. Man and ape indeed had much in common.

"Where you see pain, I see hope, power, a future for many. So you see, it is still possible that good can still come from the pain you see. Its suffering will be for a good cause." Babak glances at another monkey watching him with a hint of sadness in its behavior. His large tough, dark hands touch the bars of an empty cage closest to him. "Do not feel alone my friend. Many of the others who work with the monkeys are starting to feel the same. I feel the chimps being in cages are getting to the women and men. The chimp's entrapment saddens and disturb their spirits. Maybe it reminds them of bad times they have survived. I don't know but... between us, it is definitely becoming a quickly growing problem."

"Babak, let me ask you something? I've been studying this place since the Professor staffed me down here and for the sake of my life, I can't figure out where those exits lead." St. Clair points to several large cave like structures inside the habitat.

"I don't know, perhaps they're for larger subjects elsewhere."

"Elsewhere?" St Clair is reminded of the well-known mysterious nature of Professor Kazimir. "What about those doors, could they possibly be connected?" He points to a set of black double doors that stuck out like a soar thumb along both sides of the floor.

"I've already said too much." Babak scratches his bristly chin and looks around for any potential witnesses; He watches a woman finish cleaning out a cell a ways down from them. "I don't know, and if I did..."

"I know, you wouldn't tell me." St. Clair smiles vaguely and strolls down two more cages. "Babak, why is the military here? Why are you guys helping us, really?"

Babak laughs and looks away. Fixing his green barrette, he sticks out his chest, places both hands behind his back and lightly stomps his foot. "Ah my friend, you know such things are confidential and cannot be discussed without going through the proper channels. But I guess since you are a part of this, I may be able to leave you with these words; What if you could save your family from war, hunger or even sickness? What if you could be immune to this pain you speak of? That my friend, is why we are here. You have company." Babak walks away, continuing on his duties as Douglas comes into view down at the other end of the corridor. "Mr. Sasson." He greets passing by.

"What does he want? Here we go." St. Clair mumbles to himself and prepares for aggravation.

"The Professor asked me to give you a hand." Douglas Sasson strolls down the center of the floor loosely.

"You can tell him I'm fine Doug. I'm wrapping things up now."

"Come on, certainly there's something I can do to help a big guy like you?" Douglas spins around and roars at one of the monkeys in a nearby cage, scaring it. The chimpanzees break into a symphony of wild cries and squawks.

"Doug, seriously? Are we going to need a leash for you? Don't do that please." St. Clair tilts his head at him oddly.

"Come on, they're just monkeys. They'll be sliced and diced in no time anyway." Douglas picks up an old grape off the floor and prepares to throw it at a cage. "For the love of science!" He beams the grape at a chimp; St Clair blocks the grape.

"Can't you be any more professional?"

"How can I be professional when you guys keep holding us back?" Douglas huffs in a low voice, dissatisfied with the rapid increase of his pay. "Look, I know you don't want me to be down here with you, but just know, I don't want to be down here with you either. I'm sick of these scientist!" Douglas kicks a cloud of dirt and gravel wildly at Hugo as he walks pass his cage.

St. Clair snatches him up by the shirt, the room fills with the loud calls of chimps banging their hands and food containers against the bars of their cells. "No you look, I'm not on your mess today Doug! I don't know what your problem is, but it's not with me. You do something like that again, and we are going to have a long talk, and not with words. Respect nature!" He shoves him back towards the center of the floor. "Now, instead of acting like animals, why don't we make ourselves more productive. Show me where those lead." He returns his focus to those curious black doors.

Straightening his clothes, Douglas spits on the ground. Pausing for a moment, St. Clair could see a thought forming in Doug's pea head. "I ain't showing you nothing." He smirks deviously. Taking a card off of his key chain, he throws it at St. Clair with force. "Show yourself, team mate."

Curving in mid-air, slightly slicing St. Clairs face, the card bounces off his cheek, he catches it in his hands. "You better be happy I like my job, boy! I'm warning you Doug, I swear... I'm not on your mess today!" Griping and fussing, the remainder of the time, St. Clair uses the key card to unlock the mysterious double doors. Stepping into a much older and shabby looking laboratory constructed mainly of concrete, his eyes shift around the room at all the animal harnesses, restraints and chain collars in sight. Used and unused medical tools fill trays and counter tops of tables and blood stained sinks around him. "What kind of unsanitary...room...is this? Most labs just make chimps available for inoculation but... this is different." Logical words escape his mouth as more solid black doors and a large and rusted dark iron cage with what appear to be large breathing holes, sit in the corner of the room, striking his curiosity. "That definitely isn't Hugo's." He comments to himself. "Phew, it stinks in here! Doug, what is this used for? Oh, never mind." He corrects himself, remembering the mood Douglas was in. Studying the container, St. Clair notices that there were no combination pads or digital locks to secure the container, only three large pins, pushed into re-enforced metal loops, locked the 12 foot container.

"You know curiosity killed the cat." Douglas eases into the entrance way, hiding a sarcastic smile underneath the dimness of the room.

"Anything in there?" St. Clair ask, receiving no response. Looking through the large circular holes, he places an ear close to the container. "Hmm?" He knocks on the cold iron surface;

nothing happens. Stepping back, he stares up at the sheer size of the container and tries to pull one of the iron pins free from the loops with no success.

Thinking of the Professors words and the conversation he was ease dropping on, Douglas suddenly gets the spark of an evil ideal. "Idiots." He taps a few keys on a computer sitting at a desk; the cage unlocks. "For science."

Debating on whether or not to address Douglas on the name calling or to quietly pursue his interest, St. Clair gives him a mean look and swings open the door of the cage. Resting the door gently against the body of the container, he peeps inside. Dark, dry and quite roomy, a foul unrecognizable stench forces an arm over his nose and mouth. "What is that smell? What on earth was in here?" On top of hay and dirt, he steps to the center of the cage and clicks on a small, silver flashlight pen. Pointing it near the inner rim, he scans around the wall of the cage. Something large breaks the beam of St. Clair's light. The cage door slams closed in a echoing clang as the sounds of the three metal pins locking alarms him. "Doug, stop playing around, open the door! Doug?" St. Clair calls out as something knocks him to the floor, shearing through his abdomen. Attacked by an unknown creature, he screams in terror, fighting back against the mauling. "Douglas!" Are the last word uttered from the cage.

Waiting a few seconds extra before calling for help, Douglas snatches the radio from his belt. "Code red in the cage! I repeat, code red in the cage! Babak, Babak, get the tranquilizers! Bring the tranq-guns!" He runs out of the room back into the opening.

OVICH 1

Upon the lingering weeks ahead, just past the native shrines that serve as testimonials to the gone but not forgotten slave trade, progression moves rapidly beneath the earth inside the secret laboratory. Professor Kazimir pushes to further prove his hypothesis that chimpanzees, gorillas, and orangutans are far more serologically similar to humans than proposed. As a result, Boris Vladimir Kazimir proposes and partakes in reproducing experiments with similar anthropoid reproductive cells that may or may not result in a hybrid beings of man and ape combined. A sense of tension and uneasiness grow and spread among the crew and military hands of the underground network of small scientist since the unknown vanishing of St. Clair. On that same fifth lower level, the Sukhumi, monkeys continue to be prepped, trained and tested for space travel at all times as well as other immoral ground breaking discoveries. The process of training six monkeys, deemed most intelligent for space travel begins, as the ones who weren't capable of their duties continue to be eliminated from the group, separated, and prepped for other scientific uses. Despite the protest and personal beliefs of Dr. Richard Adler and Abigail Lapin, the Professor, whom always have had their best interest, with the help of Douglas Sasson on his side, still manages to coach them into moving forward in the name of science.

Down the poorly lit corridors of the Ovich 1 floor, army boots busily clunk and scuff against the tiled floor, as a light dusting

171

of military hands transport animals and medical equipment quickly towards their specific destinations. Rabbits and guinea pigs squeal as they are lifted by the scruffs of their necks and switched from cages in the center of the floor. A mixed breed of horses, cows, bison and donkeys kick and huff at the steel rails of their mobile enclosures being pushed across the halls; each rushed to be prepped for cross breeding. The animals all sense something not right in air as the loud cries of raging monkeys bounce off the walls around them. Connected to rooms of chimpanzees chained to beds and various monitoring machines, the dark, secret insemination lab of Professor Kazimir is in full operation. Evolving from science fiction to an evidence based practice, the Heavens Gate Center was instrumental in the studies of the human heart and lung during and after transplant. Reaching several levels of success, Kazimir and his team swiftly move from head and brain transplants, to spinal chord repair and stimulation research. From there, Kazimir proposes a human chord linkage formula which doesn't get the proper green light from his sponsors, and his attempt to eliminate human diseases without cure through the newly discovered process appear to go on the back burner for the time being. Angered by the decisions of his investors, Kazmir gathers his team and launches forward into his next venture of extreme surgery.

"On Patient X… hmm, let's go with the catheter. I think we'll try a IUI (intrauterine insemination) with this one. Patient G, we'll go with a traditional ICI (intracervical insemination). Prepare the syringes please." Professor Kazimir orders as he walks bedside of his strapped, unconscious apes; each placed dorsally recumbent, on a holding apparatus with their pelvis slightly raised. "We're going to use this method to try to increase the pregnancy rate. We need the purest sample, Mrs. Lapin if you will." He hints to Abigail to prepare the pre-washed sperm samples.

Removing a gas mask from the patient, Abigail watches the movement of the old man and the actions of the extra hands around their party in the corner of her eye; feeling something was fishy. She stares down at an 8 cm long sterile catheter attached to a 1 ml syringe. "Somethings not right." Abigail whispers to Richard. "Professor... isn't the act of natural reproduction just as efficient? Is this necessary?" Thinking of all the twist to the other experiments they've tried in the back of her mind, she knew there was something extra they had to be partaking in for the professor. Abigail attempts to pinpoint it.

Professor Kazimir stops in place, the entire room seem to pause in slow motion. "In doubt again, Mrs Lapin? You're mighty late with your questions this time, aren't you? I assure you; there is no difference between fertilization procedures. It just gives me more personal reassurance, and... it gives us great practice." He smiles and proceeds on checking the beds of sedated monkeys around them. "There are many things we're going to learn from this."

Having retrieved six vials from the mini-cryopreservation tank, each pulled from a special smoking container of liquid nitrogen and placed on a Dry Heat Block; Abigail mixes them by inversion several times and places them in a pre-warming counting chamber, analyzed and evaluated by Dr. Richard Adler. Abigail stares down at one of the vials oddly. Labeled with an anonymous title, date and a unique number recorded on its side, she examines it. "Hmm. That's unusual." Counting the digits, she instantly realizes that it had more numbers than required. Before she could speak on the matter, Richard had already spotted something on his computer.

"Uhh... this can't be right. Everything seems to be normal, temperatures perfectly heated, but... the sperm count of the sample is way lower than it should be." Richard mutters low into the computer monitor. "The sperm count is lower than two other species I know. This can't be a chimp." He retrieves more information from the identification numbers on the vials.

"Hey guys, have any of you seen St. Clair, he's been gone for some days now, isn't he apart of the team?" Nikita Ho Chi Minh interrupts them; her wide slanting eyes stare over her face mask at them with concern. "He hasn't been in his room. His bed has been the same for weeks."

"Begin inseminations." Professor Kazimir blows a whistle, instructing the room to proceed.

"It's human." Richard closely studies the data from one of the sperm samples.

"What?" Abigail nearly loses her composure.

"Good old St. Clair... I think he was fired, terminated. I dunno, heard he messed up an important shipment of medicine or something?" Overhearing, Douglas eases next to Nikita and attempts to cover his trail with lies. "What did you hear?"

"So why didn't he tell us, if he was fired? The Professor knows we're family and St. Clair is one of us. It's not like the Professor to do something like that. I know he'd want to be here. This is all he talked about." Nikita continues to check the vital signs of the chimp in front of her while trying her best to keep her voice down. "Somethings up."

"What's wrong with you guys? This is big business. This is our time! What are you doing? Focus, we don't have time for this." Douglas tries to cease their conversation. "Just do what you're told and keep your mouths shut! We're here to do a job and to go home."

"Rich?" Abigail watches the military hands around them begin inseminations.

"Okay, I'll say something." Richard stands up from the computer. "Wait, stop, time out! Everyone, everything, I'm sorry, stop. Professor Kazimir!" Douglas runs over to him and tries to stop him. "The samples are contaminated! Testing, says they're human." Richard gets the professors attention and shoves Douglas out the way.

Professor Kazimir sighs and slowly walks back in their direction. "Yes," He inhales and exhales a long puff of warm wind. "The samples are human, Richard. I don't understand. I told you before, it's all legal."

"We've talked about this before, Professor. What are you trying to do here, why are you mixing humans with monkeys? It doesn't work!" Richard argues. "I will not... we cannot support these immoral experiments any longer."

"Immoral? Ha!" Kazimir laughs loudly. "Why, because I propose that antropoide cells could be similar enough to result in a hybrid between humans and other apes? Look, lets stop the games. Many can benefit from this including the military. A new being has already been created, I want to duplicate that science. Why not create a new man, invincible, insensitive to pain, resistant?"

"An invincible human? A super soldier is more like it? It all make sense now. That's why the military is here. You're planning to grow them soldiers aren't you? Boris, you're a mad man." Richard looks into the eyes of the Professor and throws his badge onto the floor.

"This is bullshit Boris!" Abigail tosses down her gloves and storms out crying as Nikita follows.

"If you quit now, you will never work a day in another laboratory again. You'll regret it!" Kazimir threatens as Richard steps quickly after the two women. He signals Douglas to stop them as a low muffled boom sounds around them, shaking the entire structure of the building. Red warning lights flash on the emergency alert system around the complex setting off loud buzzing sirens. "What on earth is going on, what is happening today?" The Professor shouts. "I swear caring for this facility is like working on a sub-marine." He references the building to a ship at war; being always subject to sinking. "Babak, what is happening down there, what was that explosion?" Total power shuts down throughout the building, Kazmir quickly snatches his walky-talky from his hip and tries to work the buttons in the dark. "Babak? Security? Can anyone answer me?"

Through the static feedback and loud screams heard on the radio, Babak's strong vocals come through. "We don't know exactly Professor but there was a breach in the Cage. All of the chimps are loose, I repeat… all the chimps are loose!"

"Incredible." Professor Kazimir shakes his head in dismay, desperately trying to figure a quick solution. "Ready the tranquilizing guns, we've got to get those backup generators working. The entire buildings in jeopardy!" He glances at the silhouette of beds, machines and military helpers in the room with him. "Momar, keep a handle on things here. Be completely ready when the power comes on." He instructs one of the nearby aides. Clicking on a flashlight fountain pen, he fumbles his way in the dark, exiting into the main hall. He hobbles pass Abigail who was standing in a huddle between Richard and Nikita.

"What was that rumble?" Asked Richard inside the loud commotion on the floor. "That was incredible."

"Sounded like something exploded underneath us, we should evacuate!" Nikita suggest, becoming in fear of her life.

"I felt it through my entire body. Look, there goes the Professor. Looks very upset. Wonder where he's off to so fast? Probably hustling to get the power back on no doubt." Abigail watches him in the dark. "He's a mad scientist."

"Hey, maybe this is our chance to get to the bottom of things and to see what he's really doing down here? The power's off." Richard shares his bright idea. "Security's down right now."

"I don't want to be a part of this. Something exploded and that's not good! We should get as far away from here as possible, we're done here anyway." Nikita, frightened, peers through the shadows of flashing red lights and scampering workers. "I'm not going to die in this test lab!"

"Nikita, it's going to be okay. Find the way back to the room and pack your things." Abigail reassures her. "We'll meet you there."

"Are you okay?" Nikita squeezes Abigail's arm.

"Yeah, I'll be alright. Thanks. You just be careful." Abigail hugs her good friend and close coworker one last time.

"You too. Both of you; Richard." Nikita steps away from them. "Hurry." She disappears into the loudness of the chaos.

CHAPTER 3

SECRETS END

Bumping into people and objects, geneticist Richard Adler and primatologist/scientist, Abigail Lapin stealthily follow Professor Kazimir through the elaborate catacomb of laboratories and medical storage areas within the Ovich 1 floor. In the power outage, they lose sight of him in a hand full of passing workers trying to find their way in the dark. In the path of armed soldiers, each equipped with flashlights, the two duck into a room admitted only for certain qualified personnel, unnoticed.

"In here." Richard whispers as he eases the door closed behind them in a low crouch. "Good, looks like all the doors are unlocked. Let's hope the others are unlocked as well."

"We lost Boris. Where do you think he's headed?" Abigail, glances around the room under the flickering red lights.

"I'm not for certain; I'd guess the cage. Maybe that's where we need to go?"

"Not until those soldiers pass. I think this is one of those areas we're definitely not suppose to be in."

"Shh, back! Someone's coming!" Richard pushes her back. As the door opens, he takes her by the hand and exits through the swinging double doors in back of the room. Pulling Abigail down an aisle of shelved interbred rodents of all kinds, Richard nudges his seeing glasses back onto his face and dashes into a unfamiliar corridor of halls and doors. In a clear, he hunches over to catch his breath. Quite out of shape, Richard takes a hard swallow;

hearing the soldiers coming behind them. "Sheesh!" Richard guides Abigail down the hall and around the corner. Quietly, he opens another door and gently shoves her into another room. There, under a metal table in the back corner, they find cover and wait. "I think we lost them." Richard feels the cold, damp surface of stones slates underneath his hands.

"Where are we now? I've lived here for months but I feel like I'm in a maze." Abigail notice there were no emergency lights along the ceiling or floor. Standing in total darkness, she searches her pockets and retrieves her flashlight pen along with Richard. "Look at this place."

"What is that smell?" Richard also rises to his feet, bumping into a table of chains and restraints. "What the heck are these for, gorillas?" He flashes his pen across at a counter top of bloody syringes and crude medical tools. "What are we, back in mid-evil times?" He bats the sound of tiny buzzing away from his ear.

"Looks like the surgeons recently left. Probably because there's no power." Stepping a few feet, Abigail's hand dips into a wet ceramic container. Shining her light down upon it, she sees flies hovering over several large bowls of mushed fruit, leaves, insects and chunks of meat. "They were feeding something." She wipes her hand against her pants leg.

"It stinks, something has to be in here with us." Richard shines his light against computers, a wall of chained leashes, keys, iron wrist and neck cuffs, and Tasers. He walks over to the far corner and opens a cabinet of medical supplies, catheters, lubrication and drainage bags. "We must be near another insemination lab. Come on, let's see if there's another way out of here. I don't think we should go the way we came. I don't want to be thrown out just yet, or shot." He smiles up under the light of his pen.

The room muffled sound from the outside as heat and water pipes knocked in the unseen corners around them. Passing old looking incubators and infusion pumps connected to steel mobile stands, they walk down the middle of the stone floor until coming to a large, black, open walkway which led to another room, much darker than the one they were already in. Entering, instantly, they cover their noses as the foul smell of chimp activity singe and bite at the inner hairs and lining of their nostrils. Through a narrow passage into another chamber, Richard and Abigail find themselves in a room of barred cages.

"Wha, what is this?" Abigail points her pen inside cage after cage of dead and dying chimpanzees. "Look at them, I think they're all female."

"How do you know?" Richard peers down at the skull and the deteriorating remains of a neglected chimp inside a cage.

"Look at them closely, they're all pregnant." She points out some of the large and most obvious features on the bodies of the chimps. "I don't think Kazimir has enough staff to cover all these operations. Look at this abuse. Sad. Clearly animal cruelty."

"Yeah, but what were they impregnated with? I thought we were the only ones inseminating?" Richard shines his light upon a metal tray sitting on a small table on wheels. The tray contains unorthodox medical equipment that he had only read about in history books. "I can't believe Kazimir is allowing someone to use these tools on anything alive." He eyes a bloody hammer, a Brad driver, holder and a large pair of rusted pliers. A used osteotome sat upon the table's edge; this hand held medical instrument was like a chain saw. A sharp spike upon it was driven into the patient's skull to hold it in place as a doctor would crank its handle to turn its mini-saw tooth blade. It was at one time, superior to a reciprocating saw and chisel, when it came to getting through a human bone without tissue damage. Inside of a yellow pale, laying next to a cell, dozens of chimpanzee teeth and fangs spilled onto the floor in front of them.

"Hmm, someone's been doing real dental work." Abigail comments with tears in her eyes. Having spent nearly a life time working with monkeys, she shows great respect and compassion for the wellbeing of the species. Her watering eyes fall short of a female chimp, barely alive in its cage. "Found a live one. Look at her. Someone's been pulling out her teeth. They can't even protect themselves from predators properly without fangs. Guess they thought their teeth was a threat to the stupid staff. Poor chimps. There are other ways to go about this! We have to shut this place down."

"Wait, are there doors on these cells? No, good, the exit doors are in the back on the inside. If there is one alive or full of energy, I wouldn't want it coming after us, thinking we're the surgeons who pulled out its teeth." Richard shines his light around the other nearby cells. Then, in complete silence, the two hear an odd noise coming from the other end of the caging area. Richard freezes in place.

Abigail's heart drops as her thoughts wander off into a dark place of wild, ferociously attacking chimpanzees fleeing from their cages. Enveloped in a sudden icy chill, "Richard," was all Abigail could utter; watching him slowly inch towards the source of the noise.

Holding out his hand as if she could see it, Richard firmly whispers, "Stay there!" and inches towards the edge of the long row of chimp cells. Upon nearing the corner, pointing the pen steady; he notices a large opening of dark space. A tough, large, pink and brown hair covered hand grabs the bar to the left of his face, causing him to jump and nearly drop his pen. "It's another one, she's alive though. Nearly gave me a heart attack!" Richard holds his chest and laughs to himself. Aiming the pen at the cell, a 3 ft tall chimp around 90 pounds, reaches for him. Flat faced, covered entirely of blackish brown hair with whiskers on its chin, the chimp makes a lip puckering face at him.

"She's worried and probably hungry. Maybe this is who they were about to feed." Abigail walks up behind him.

"Has all her teeth. Hey, look at this." He flashes the pen onto the far wall of the open space, illuminating another wall of chimpanzees confined in metal containers, some with windows, other's without. "Holy cow, he's conducting conditioning experiments too!" Richard points to different sized restrictive chambers positioned along the wall. He noticed that each metal box had an outside manual locking mechanism on them which reassured their safety once more.

"Why would he do this? Sick bastard!" Abigail shines her light at the visible imprisoned chimps separated from their group, sadly in disgust.

"Oh-my-goodness, what is this? No!" Richard cleans his glasses with the cuff of his shirt and fumbles them back onto his nose. Sweating, he nervously shines light into the corner on his left, a green, futuristic designed pod able to accommodate ten people comes into view. Walking up to the structure, he wipes his hand across its large dirty window and peeps inside. The size of a large sauna, the large structure housed the remains of three dead species inside. The bone structure and bodily features indicated that whatever it was, was neither man nor chimp, but a combination of both. "He did it. I mean they're not living, but he did it! Kazimir created a hybrid."

"Behind our backs too. Scum." Abigail snarls into the window beside him. "Who were the donors?"

"Come on, let's get out of here and find this guy." Richard turns away.

"What do you have planned, I mean, what can we really do?" Abigail stares into the darkness of the huge space in the opposite corner.

"We have our proof now. That's all we need. He's broken way too many protocols. A few calls to the big Willies will shut him down for good. Or... do it ourselves." Exclaims Richard, beginning to step away.

"Yeah, let's go. I don't even want to know what's in that one." Abigail takes her light off of an even bigger container sitting in the opposite corner. Catching up to Richard, she takes hold to the back of his open lab coat with one hand, to help guide her in the dark. A loud metal door closes behind them. Spinning around, Abigail shines her pen wildly in all directions. "What was that?"

"You heard it too, humph? I think we need to go." Richard walks backwards, waving his pen like a magic wand in front of him. "I don't see anything."

Before he could finish the sentence, something else moved inside the darkness with them. Pointing in the direction of the far wall, a short childlike figure moves into light of Abigail's pen. Stumbling out as if just waking up, the small person lowers a set of long arms, which extends pass its legs onto the floor. Holding something in its hand, a humanoid looking creature covered in long dark scraggly hair, throws down a clump of vegetation onto the stone floor between them. A thick fold of brow-less muscle borders its forward facing, reflective eyes glare, as miss-shaped human like ears protrude from the sides of its small round head. A pudgy and mashed in, human nose with an elongated form sniffs the air curiously in the darkness before them. Scratching its unseen belly, it picks up an unwanted scent and a sour taste in the wind. The creature's blood soaked lips press tightly together under Richards light, indicating to Abigail that it was ready to attack. It barks loudly in their direction, smacking the floor, batting at its chest.

"It's a hybrid, go!" Abigail tells Richard as they hit the corner and dash for the lab and the door they came from. The hybrid beast, half man and part chimp, charges after them.

"He's done it, I can't believe he's done it. An actual hybrid... is chasing us!" Richard takes Abigail's hand and slings her in front of him as Kazimir's creation leaps on his back, tackling him to the floor. Feeling his hand hit a metal post, in the darkness, Richard grabs hold of the leg of a mobile, metal table, and bats the mixed primate off.

Sliding backwards, in split seconds, in two hops, the creature leaps onto Abigail, pinning her to the bars of the female chimpanzee's cells. Her face, rammed and smashed up against the white painted bars, Abigail screams in absolute horror. As a clump of her hair is yanked back, a massive plug is pulled out, freeing her head. Folding into a ball, Abigail desperately dodges its snapping jaws of missing teeth, managing to kick the hybrid in the face several times. "Richard!" She calls out; her flashlight, L.E.D. pen snaps and crunches into pieces under her knee. In pitch black, the hybrid seizes her by the wrist with its foot and drags her across the floor. Feeling the heavy weight and awesome force of the creature press down into her back, Abigail felt the skin and muscle being bit from the side of her face as she is struck swiftly from behind.

Shining light across the floor, Richard spots the large rusty pliers. The size of a small pocket knife, the osteotome also lay next to the cell of the healthier chimp. He grabs the pliers and quickly snatches the osteotome before the chimp-man mistaken it for food or a toy object. The hybrid screams violently as Richard quickly pinpoints its position in the dark. "Abigail, hold on!" He hears her scream cut off abruptly ahead. In the same hand as the pliers, he shines the pen forward. In the first single glimpse of the hybrid creature, Richard launches bravely forward in high spirits of saving his friend and colleague, Abigail Lapin. Using his large size, Richard rams the ape-man from over her. And in a scuffle of courage against the primitive brute, strength, claws and teeth clash against balled fist and tools. Richard thrusts the osteotome into its side and seizes the creature by its thin neck. Scratched and kicked, he shakes off the blows by the four hands of the hybrid, forcefully beating the large steel pliers into its head until its neck snaps inside his large shaking hand. Continuing to strike the creature several more times until he felt its body had completely stopped moving, Richard is pulled from away from behind. Pushing away wildly, he prepares to die fighting as Abigail's soft hands wraps warmly around his body. He tosses down the pliers, it clangs against the floor next to the leg of the hybrid, loudly. They stand in a subtle silence at the mercy of the remaining caged chimps kept alive, in the clutches of the tiny ticking of pipes hidden around the walls; relieved, crying. "Abigail." He hugs her.

Since the power was out and the elevators were down, on the other side of the floor, Nikita Ho Chi Minh scurries down the hall leading to a single stairwell upstairs, adjacent to another stairwell leading down. Inside the large hall, under the flashing red alert lights and fleeing frantic military aides, scared, she stops and leans against the wall. Peering straight down the hall, down into a large, spiral stairwell, terrible screams of people and indescribable, animalistic howls belch from the stairwell. Cringing to the wall, Nikita witness the shadows of apes and injured people, pouring from up out the stairway. Screaming at the tops of her lungs at the sight of two chimpanzees running pass her, she presses flat against the wall and slides to the door leading to the stairwell upstairs. As two African women run up the stairs ahead of her, swiftly Nikita slips inside the open door and closes it all the way. Only able to go up, she staggers up the dark steps onto the next floor, the Gemini. Unable to reach the Galley floor upstairs from that stairwell, Nikita hurries through the third level which was a ring of connecting labs and storage areas. Dogs with the upper torso, front legs and head of puppies on their backsides, roam the floors and halls freely like demonic hell hounds under the red lights and sirens. Workers shove and bump into each other in a panic around her; as if in a bad dream, she pushes onward under the falling dust and paint chips that tumble from the ceilings as something large rattles and forces its way through the vents over her head. On the floor that she regularly worked, she enters an empty laboratory and retrieves a flashlight from a known emergency supply cabinet. Deciding to exit out of a side door into another hall, she shutters at the horrific yells and horrible sounds heard throughout the building.

"What are you doing, what are you up too? And where's our little friends, Abigail and Dr. Adler? I know they're somewhere around hiding." Douglas grabs her from behind, Nikita snatches away. "Oh, they're not around. What's wrong, you don't miss me? No one's around." He smiles devilishly, placing both hands up in the beam of her flashlight.

"In your dreams! I don't have to tell you anything!" Nikita tries to walk off as Douglas grabs her by the arm.

"Wait a minute. You're not going anywhere. You know something." Douglas pulls her close and places both arms around her. "Give me a little kiss baby, it's just me and you."

"Pucker up." Nikita hugs him tight. Leaning in close, she headbutts him, breaking his nose, then kicking him between the legs, she brings Douglas helplessly to his knees.

"Wait, Nikita!" He yells out.

Nikita takes the light off of him and turns away. Raising the flashlight, she suddenly halts in place as dozens of chimpanzees surround them. Backing against the wall, Nikita forces her small body into the closet door. Slamming it behind her and running hard, she hears the chimps slam into the door as Douglas screams on the other side. Chimps break into the room wildly behind her. Calling to the others in their group, the monkeys ransack everything as Nikita runs for her life through the laboratories and halls. Flinching at the sight of rabbits and mice running loosely between her feet, she notices the shades of their heads and bodies were two different colors, indicating that they were transplant subjects. A woman darts in front of her, hollering with severe injuries to her face, Nikita turns her head in fright and pushes through a large silver door. Inside a room where dogs and perhaps various horses were bred, she thinks of the fastest way to get to the Galley. Still in darkness, drained, she pushes on, as a faint cry catches her attention. Listening close, she makes out the vocal tones to be human. Guessing that someone was probably injured from an animal attack, she builds the nerves to ignore and leave them. Yet, her good conscience stops her, she prepares her queasy stomach for things she might not normally be able to handle or see. Following the cry to a heavy, white reinforced door with a tinted looking window, she opens it.

Inside a dark room of jarred specimen, oxygen tanks and medical devices, under a giant lamp, an unimaginable product of a heinous act, stirs upon a hospital bed. Nikita shines her flashlight upon the mattress. In crinkled, bloodied linen, connected to tubes and wires; William, the disabled gentlemen whom the professor claim to have invited when she first arrived, lay on the sheets naked, foaming at the mouth, twitching, dying from seizures. Attached to the lower portion of his neck and upper back by stitches and a special bonding agent, the head of St. Clair blinks and full lips slightly move as if trying to speak. She screams in fright, unable to fully comprehend or take in completely what she was looking at. "St. Clair?" Is all she could utter, unable to enter the room all the way. She stands in the doorway, bursting into tears. "No, no. How could they do this? No!" In disbelief, Nikita Ho Chi Minh stares at the shadow of her former friend on the bed as the door shuts. Sobbing uncontrollably, an eerie clicking across an aluminum or a tin surface startles her. Softening her cry, an increase in tapping forces her to listen attentively. Becoming more paranoid, nervously she shines her flash light around the room of animal cages and pens. Jittery, she trembles with the light, twirling in circles. A loud crash sends her jumping to the side and the flashlight tumbling to the floor. Swiftly dropping down, she finds the flashlight turned off. Flicking it on, except for a white beard, a large hairless face gazes directly into the pit of her fears. A chimp, in hunt mode, releases a strange call that could be heard for two miles around. Starving and showing its fangs, the primate charges at her in a range of wild hoots and monkey shrieks. Nikita, hollering for dear life, tries to quickly evade the attack while receiving multiple lacerations to the face and body. Tripping over her own foot, she falls to the hard floor, chipping her front teeth. A clan of five or more large chimpanzees pounce down on her from the open vent that ran across the ceiling, each joining in on the tasty feast.

Two floors down, on the lowest level, the Sukhumi, the sprinkler system shuts off after successfully dousing out pockets of large fires around the floor. Under dripping water, a thin film of smoke drifts through the pitch black halls of yelling, screams and strange animal sounds. Almost completely abandoned, Richard and Abigail creep out of a side stairway onto the floor. Disregarding plans to find the Professor due to their injuries, they stagger on their feet in search of a alternate way out.

"Those monkeys are blocking all the exits! I've never been this far down before, there has to be another way to the surface from here." Richard, resting Abigail's arm over his shoulder, looks down at his flickering pen. "Batteries dying."

"Wait, aim the light over there. Look!" She directs him to the deceased body of a man, slumped over, wearing a head lamp.

Not wanting to touch the man's blood saturated clothes, Richard eases down and removes the lamp from the victims head. "I think my shoulder is dislocated..." Battered and bruised, he puts the head lamp on with one hand and powers it on. "Ouch, my rib is cracked too. How's that leg, can you make it?"

"Ankles still twisted, but I'll manage." Abigail touches the blood seeping down the back of her head and neck. Suffering from multiple bites and deep puncture wounds, she rips a strip of cloth from her clothes and holds it over a gash on her shoulder. "Where to now?"

"Guess we should follow the bodies and mess." Richard stands facing a path of papers and medical equipment thrown everywhere. "Geesh, how many chimps did he capture from the forest? All of them? We have to avoid those things."

"Looks like he didn't have a big enough staff to care for them after all. Look at their behavior, it's not their fault, clearly they were neglected and way underfed. We should of just let them be." Abigail hobbles beside Richard, acting as a look out person.

Room upon room, laboratory after laboratory they entered, each appeared to be trashed and damaged by the escaped family of primates. Then, walking into the area in which the water heaters exploded, through a large hole in the wall, they hear yelling and screaming as Professor Kazimir comes into view. Stepping out the hole, Richard and Abigail see scientist and soldiers alike, scrambling and fleeing while a few struggle to preserve and save sensitive data and equipment. Suddenly, in a tremendous roar and loud gun fire, a creature only seen and heard in mythology, emerges from the shadows, sending sets of men slamming against the walls and floor in its path. Over seven feet tall, a large, hairy, bipedal ape-like creature covered in dark reddish hair runs by Richard and Abigail.

Barely able to pronounce a word, in a very muffled and deep voice, the creature growls out, "Leave me free!" As the soldiers open rounds of bullets and tranquilizers upon the monster it gallops off down the hall, disappearing somewhere within the vicinity.

"It talks?" Not knowing if he should continue on trying to save the secret laboratory or go after the intriguing specimen that just ran by, Professor Kazimir stands in the middle of the floor speechless as Babak approaches him.

"Professor, we must evacuate immediately!" He walks up angrily.

"Babak, you know I can't do that. I have too much at stake." Professor Kazimir responds, watching a soldier tranquilize a chimpanzee hanging on the ceilings light fixture.

"You have too much at stake? Professor Kazimir, your project is a failure, you knew there was a chance of this happening, something going wrong! Did you see that? That was not an ape Professor! That, that thing, your little pet... Sasquatch, just murdered four of my best trained, and injured six of my men! Not to mention the countless destruction these wild chimpanzees have made of everything! Workers are protesting against the military outside. This was not part of our agreement Professor! I'm aborting this chaos. I'm withdrawing my men from this place. You, are on your own! May GOD help you all. Pull out, everybody out, now!" Babak orders his men on the radio, turning his back totally on Professor Kazimir. "You and your team have fifteen minutes to evacuate, then I'm returning for our injured. Everything dies Professor, along with everyone who isn't us." He forewarns him before storming away completely.

"Guess your luck has ran out." Professor Kazimir hears Richards voice behind him. "Ah, I knew you wouldn't leave me." He turns around to the sight of two of his most valuable employees, dirty and clothes ripped, dripping of blood. "Goodness, look at you two. You survived. Where's Douglas and Nikita?"

"Where's St. Clair?" Abigail sharply ask with hate in her eyes.

"St. Clair? Oh…" Kazimir's eyes widen, he looks away as two other scientist from another one of his secret groups dart by.

"This not worth it, man!" one of the young scientist, wearing the expression of desperation on his smut smudged face, rushes by dropping a box of files and miscellaneous objects.

"Oh? What do you mean, oh? Where's our friend, St. Clair?" Abigail points a taser that she collected from the hybrid room between his legs. "The truth, no bull, Boris!"

"Wait, okay, please! No!" Pleads the Professor as Abigail applies slight pressure to his crotch area. "Truth! He, he was doing some research and was fatally injured. I had no choice but to preserve him!"

"Preserve him? What does that even mean? What did you do, Boris?"

"How was he fatally injured? What kind of research was he doing?" Richard interrupts, not believing a word.

"He, he was working in the cage and something got loose, something escaped and attacked him. I don't know the exact details, I wasn't there. I, I was just called to the scene, I swear."

"Something got loose? What do you mean, something?

Something like what, what got to St. Clair, Boris?" Richard grabs him by the collars as the 7ft giant creature the soldiers were chasing, inched thirty feet behind the professor, approaching. Eyeing the monster munching on the head of the scientist that just passed them, Richard eyes shift to the small group of chimpanzees that followed behind it. "Get us out of her, or I'm leaving you to your works." Richard spins Professor Kazimir around to see what was coming after them.

"Oh... th... th, that's what got loose! No, please?" Professor Kazimir shutters at the sight of the rapidly approaching primates. "Goodness gracious, we must hurry quickly!"

"Then move!" Richard yells, shoving him ahead.

The professor steps off with urgency. "The chimps have blown the breakers, the generators are totally burned out. One of the tanks exploded on a maintenance vehicle collapsing both damn transport tunnels. We'll have to take the emergency transport lift that runs through the center of the building, or else go through those things. However, it only goes to the second level." Ducking into a storage room a few feet away, he closes the door and manually locks it behind them.

"The Galley. That's a good thing, right? Then all we'd have to do is make it to the office level." Richard glances at Abigail from the corner of his eye.

"An emergency transport lift? How will that do us any good if the powers out?" Abigail hops behind him, holding on to Richard.

"It has its own power. Along with the power to the emergency system, those are the only generators working in the building." Professor Kazimir quickly accesses a computer on a wall in the room and begins copying information to a memory stick.

"What are you doing? No, we're not repeating this!" Richard snatches the stick, tosses it down and stomps it into pieces. "To the transport lift, now!" He instructs as Abigail silently enforces his words by holding the taser up to the professor's neck.

Through the back halls of the Astro-chimp testing facility,

where various primates were tested for space travel, the three elude more chimpanzee's rambling in the labs by escaping into Kazimir's unknown secret rooms throughout the main corridor. Sneaking pass hungry, curious and scared roaming chimpanzees, they take no time in reaching the transport lift. Minutes later, the three stand side by side in the lift as it climbs the floors of the building at a moderate pace. Watching the walls drop by them under the yellow lights screwed into the railings, the pulleys click and gyrate the floor beneath their feet, as they rise vertically up the shaft.

"This is it. We get Nikita, grab our things and get the heck out of here. Pardon me Boris." Richard quickly snatches of a piece of the Professors coat and dresses Abigail's ankle with it.

"So, since we have a little personal time, get to the St. Clair story. What happened?" She leans against the railing, taser in hand. She itches to hear any wrong word slip out of the Professors mouth.

"There is really nothing more I can say. I tried my best to save him. He was attacked and nearly shredded to pieces by one of the patients. I had to preserve him or let him die, I chose not to lose him." Professor Boris Kazimir eases his hand into his lab coat pocket.

"Okay, that's it right there. It's that phrase, that word... how. How was he preserved, Boris?" exclaims Richard.

"Enlighten us." Adds Abigail.

"Due to the severity of his injuries, he had to be... and could only be preserved through isolation and... transplantation." Kazimir presses the up button on a small yellow control panel hanging on the inside of the lift, nervously dripping sweat from his temples.

"Isolation and transplantation? You bastard, what are you saying? He was a good human being! You transplanted him into what?" The mere thought of St. Clair experiencing anything said, makes Richard ill all over. He stands angered as they approach the Galley level.

"We transplanted his head to the body of a temporary host, a human of course, but only until we found a healthy donor!" The Professor steps back as Abigail clicks the taser between them. "No, stop! You'll still need me to open the main security doors! They're on emergency lock down, everyone who don't know the code should be waiting there as well! You know this to be true, Dr. Adler."

"Boris?" Abigail stops him from talking; the lifts stops and opens to a dark, powerless floor. "We want your word that you will shut this little mad-cap operation down for good and discontinue this forever. It's not worth it Boris, look at the losses."

"And if I don't agree to you're little terms, then what? What will happen?"

"We will fight you the whole way and insure that you... will go to jail for a long time." Richard, knowing the bases of the legal side of things, answers for her.

"In the name of science." The Professor holds up one side of his lab coat with his hand in the pocket, firing two shots into both of them from his hidden gun through his jacket. Dropping both scientist, he presses the down button on the yellow box, coldly sending the lift back down to the lowest level. "Sorry, but I need to fix this. You may now join St, Clair in heaven. Rest in peace my friends." He places the hand holding the pistol over his heart and watches Richard and Abigail's bodies disappear into the darkness of the cavern remorsefully.

As the emergency alert sirens come back into listening range, Kazimir creeps up a narrow passageway, stepping out from behind a revolving wall panel, just near the sleeping quarters. With the coast appearing seemingly clear, he reaches into his inside shirt pocket and pulls out a hand full of memory sticks. Convinced that the worst of his worries were behind him, Professor Kazimir grins at his handful of saved documents and research. Hearing something scurrying in the next room, he stuffs the flash drives back into his shirt and draws his gun. Adjusting his head lamp, he flicks it off to avoid drawing attention. Blindly feeling his way to the nearest intersecting hall, the Professor turns back on the light, startled by the sight of a tall familiar face lurking a few feet away. Still in restraining straps, with IV and drainage lines dangling from the arm, legs and groin area, Ivan, the human brain implanted into the head of a monkey that he once kept alive on display, now lurched from the darkness before him, surgically bonded to the top of a naked body of a male human. Sprinkled of strange liquids and dabbed of blood and matter collected from throughout the facility, the hazel eyed entity staggers bare footed across the floor, leaving a trail of red from its cut and gashed feet. Scared out his wits, yet captivated by the beauty of his most recent experiment, the Professor aims his gun at the man- partial ape being, and fires. The gun jams in Kazimir's hand as Ivan knocks him to the floor with a single swing of natural enhanced strength, perching over his body in a fearsome growl. Gazing deep into the old man's soul, Ivan's big brown eyes seem to recognize and connect with Kazimir under the brightness of his head lamp.

"No, no, look, at me. That's right, friends, I'm your friend. Your... your master. It's me, the Professor, you dumb creature! Listen to me, that's right, focus. I know some intelligence is in there! Come on, that's right, you know me. Keep looking at me. Don't... kill me." The memory sticks spill from the Professors shirt pocket as he tries to calm and tame his escaped experiment in a low whisper, in fear of accidentally provoking it.

Ivan leans down mere inches away from his face, smelling the heavy breathes of fear on his lips. He speaks. "I... am Ilya... Ivanov." A deep dragging sound slurs into raspy words that spray saliva over the side of Kazimir's quivering cheeks.

"No, impossible, it can't be." The name registers in Kazimir's mind as he remembers a former scientist from the 1930's who conducted similar inseminating experiments in hopes of creating an inhumanly strong prototype worker. He feels his heart failing, Professor Kazimir is having a heart attack. He tries to grab his chest as the creature pins his arm down against the floor.

"You... will be my last... and final ex... exper...iment. In... th... the name... of... science." A burst of gruesome hollers and screams fill the hall as Ivan's sharp, fanged teeth chomp down on Boris's neck. As the Professors white shirt and coat is soaked in red, his body is dragged and hauled off mercilessly, somewhere back inside the smoking complex of Heaven's Gate. In splashes of their own blood, Professor Boris Kazimir and his remaining team of scientist, and the proof of his research, is taken by their own experiments. Silenced, covered up and never to be heard from, nor to be seen again in our lifetime, the events that happened are forgotten and erased from the pages of history. Yet history, when forgotten, always seem to have a nasty and awful habit of repeating and living again.

-end-

Printed in the United States
By Bookmasters